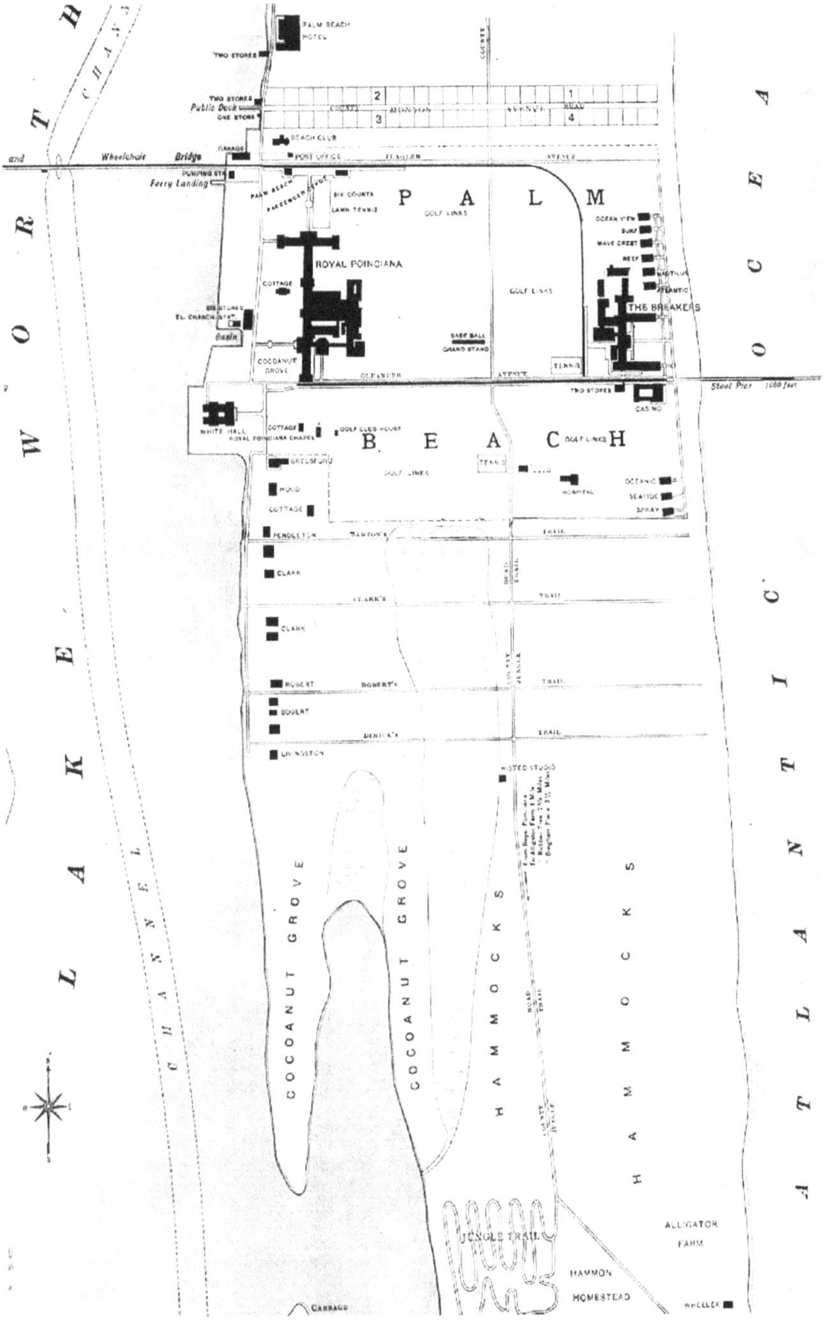
LAKE WORTH
CHANNEL
ATLANTIC OCEAN
PALM BEACH
PALM BEACH HOTEL
TWO STORES
Public Dock
ONE STORE
BEACH CLUB
POST OFFICE
GARAGE
and Wheelchair Bridge
PUMPING STA
Ferry Landing
PALM BEACH PASSENGER DEPOT
SIX COURTS LAWN TENNIS
GOLF LINKS
ROYAL POINCIANA
COTTAGE
SIX STORES
EL. CHURCH STAT.
Basin
COCOANUT GROVE
OLEANDER AVENUE
BASE BALL GRAND STAND
TENNIS
OCEAN VIEW
SURF
WAVE CREST
REEF
NAUTILUS
ATLANTIC
THE BREAKERS
Steel Pier 1000 feet
CASINO
WHITE HALL
ROYAL POINCIANA CHAPEL
GOLF CLUB HOUSE
BRELSFORD
HOOD
HOSPITAL
OCEANIC
SEASIDE
SPRAY
PENDLETON
BARTON'S TRAIL
CLARK
CLARK'S TRAIL
ROBERT
ROBERT'S TRAIL
BOGERT
DIMICK'S TRAIL
LIVINGSTON
HISTED STUDIO
COUNTY ROAD
COUNTY JUNGLE TRAIL
COCOANUT GROVE
HAMMOCKS
JUNGLE TRAIL
HAMMON HOMESTEAD
ALLIGATOR FARM
WHEELER
CABBAGE

# VI°LET

## AT THE BREAKERS

A N°VELLA

BYR°N GRUSH

Published in the United States by Broadhorn Publishing, Delavan, WI

ISBN-10: 0-692-74965-9
ISBN-13: 978-0-692-74965-4

# 1

## The Breakers

Violet was a precocious twelve year-old but took care not to be perceived as "cheeky" by the adults in her young life: Mother, Father, Grampa Andrews and Auntie Kate. She was vigilant in her self-assigned duty of custodian and chaperone to her younger sisters, Rose and Gladys, during those times when Mother had one of her headaches. In the morning she helped set the breakfast table with spoons and bowls, a pitcher of fresh milk and the box of Shredded Wheat with the picture of the rambling Shredded Wheat factory at Niagara Falls, which Violet imagined was a castle complete with knights in shining armor. After school she entertained Rose and Gladys as best she could, often resorting to a game of hide and seek when her sisters became bored with Chinese Checkers or Lincoln Logs.

This morning, Violet was surprised when Mother informed the girls they wouldn't be going to school that day. Hazel Valentine announced that the family was to embark on a spur of the moment sojourn to the fabulous luxury hotel, The Breakers, at Palm Beach. It was a blustery March in 1925, and it seemed a strange time for a trip to the beach, but Violet was exited by the prospect. The opportunity to exchange the clammy cold spring of Brooklyn for the silver sand and brilliant sun of Florida delighted her. She could hardy contain her enthusiasm as she pushed her new swim suit into the suitcase between socks and pinafore, so she broke into the little song she liked to sing when she was the most happy:

*I wish I was a mole in the ground.*
*Yes, I wish I was a mole in the ground.*
*For if I was a mole in the ground,*
*I'd root that mountain down,*
*And I wish I was a mole in the ground.*

But Violet was further surprised to learn that the impromptu vacation didn't include Dad. When she asked her mother why this was so she received a cold stare and a command to hurry and finish packing. Oh, Violet thought to herself, I suppose he must need to go to the office today. Certainly he would join them later. But why hadn't Mother just explained that to her? Adults were often mysterious and difficult to understand.

The Breakers Hotel was a sprawling four-story edifice of freshly painted wood constructed to look like an early colonial building. The original hotel, called the Palm Beach Inn, was build in 1896 by oil and railroad magnate Henry Morrison Flagler, near the grounds of his Royal Poinciana Hotel on the island of Palm Beach. The Poinciana faced the Lake Worth Lagoon, but the Palm Beach Inn fronted on the Atlantic Ocean, and soon overtook the other hotel in popularity. Unfortunately, it burned to the ground in 1903. The newly rebuilt inn was renamed The Breakers Hotel after the white-capped waves that rolled in to lap against the sandy beach.

The Breakers contained over four hundred rooms which in season would be peopled with the rich and the infamous in equal quantities. It wasn't unusual to be rubbing elbows with Vanderbilts,

Rockefellers, or Astors, and it was rumored that notorious gangsters from Chicago and Detroit spent their time in the sun at The Breakers. One celeb du jour that second week of March was none other than William Hale Thompson who was known as "Big Bill" back in Chicago. Big Bill had been the mayor of the City of the Big Shoulders until a couple of years ago and would be again, with the help of his friend, Alphonse Capone. He would go down in history as the most corrupt politician Chicago had ever known, and Chicago had known plenty. Now he was on vacation.

Motor cars were not allowed on the property, perhaps ironic since the owner and builder of the hotel was an oil tycoon—but Flagler ran a spur line from his Florida East Coast Railroad to bring guests right across Lake Worth on a trestle, linking the hotel to the coastal railway. Violet and her family traveled up the broad, palm-lined approach in a large wheeled chair propelled by an attached bicycle. The brisk ocean breeze ruffled Violet's hair, recently bobbed by special permission from Mother on the occasion of Violet's last birthday. As she got her first glimpse of the imposing structure of the hotel she immediately thought of the picture on the cereal box. Now she had arrived at her very own castle!

Mother charged Violet with the responsibility of overseeing Rose and Gladys once they arrived at the hotel's lobby. Predictably, the two girls scattered in opposite directions once they had cleared the heavy wooden entry doors. Not another game of hide and seek—not now, thought Violet.

The clatter of two sets of patent leather Mary Janes reverberated in the immense lobby, a cavernous chamber carved from the fantasies of a former century: polished oak panels, mural-sized paintings of ancient wars, crystal chandeliers that would have dazzled mad King Ludwig, elaborate Arabian carpets and exotic potted plants from Brazilian rain forests. Violet found Gladys hanging on the edge of a pedestal table which held a flower-filled jardiniére decorated, and this seemed to be the attraction for Gladys, with nymphs and satyrs engaged in exuberant merrymaking. Envisioning the tipping of the table, the thunderous crash and resultant barrage of pottery fragments and dirt clods like an artillery bombardment, Violet yanked Gladys away from her precarious position and turned to search for Rose.

She spotted Rose across the room talking to a man who was

seated at a grand piano on a long wooden piano bench. Gladys was only six but Rose was ten and surely should know better than to talk to strangers! With Gladys in tow, Violet hurried to the rescue of the errant Rose. The man, dressed immaculately in double-breasted vest, wide lapelled suit jacket and baggy flannel pants was the personification of a jazz era icon. He began playing a song which Violet recognized as "Yes, We have No Bananas." This was apparently at the request of Rose, who bounced excitedly like a new puppy.

Violet stood for a moment and studied the man. The skin of his face was smooth and tanned—no, not so much tanned as deeply olive in color. Violet imagined him a swarthy Sheik of Arabia, a Persian Prince or an Egyptian dignitary, visiting her castle on some ominous mission. Then the man turned his head to glance down at Violet and she saw the small scar over his left eyebrow.

Violet, still holding on to Gladys with one hand, collected Rose with the other and pulled both girls away. Mother was headed toward the elevator. Violet managed to drag her sisters into the elevator just as the brass door, decorated with the angular, abstracted shapes of a tropical island, closed behind them.

Violet loved to ride in elevators. This one, resplendent with beveled glass mirrors and brass trim had a glorious panel of buttons to push and a row of numbers that lit up with a ruby red glow when you passed each floor. One, two, three—fouth floor. Ding. She loved the low hum and slow vibration of the box as it crept its way upward, swaying ever so slightly.

But the greatest thing about hotels, according to Violet, was the hallways. Vast labyrinths carpeted in garish curlicues of fronds you seemed to fall into as you wandered, wondering where each branching might lead. The mysterious stacks of dirty dishes or pairs of shoes outside closed doors whose keyholes cried out to you to press your eye to them. Hallways that beckoned you to run with joyous abandonment when Mother turned you loose to your own devices. Hallways that wound endlessly through your temporary castle, high above the white-capped waves.

And so, once Mother had curled up on the settee with Rose and Gladys and an Uncle Wiggly picture book, Violet asked, "Mummy, may I go exploring?" Hazel knew her daughter to be a sensible young girl, not prone to mischief...at least, not the hazardous kind...and so she gave Violet a sweet smile and a nod and off Violet went for an adventurous escapade up and down the sprawling corridors of The Breakers Hotel.

As Violet traversed the hallway she alternated right and left turns at intersections, a practice resulting in her discovery of several dead ends. She then retraced her steps and took the opposite turning. The gilt-framed oil portraits of women dressed in high Victorian fashion which lined the walls fascinated her. She began to notice that rooms were numbered evenly on one side of the hall and had odd numbers on the other. Curious. As she passed rooms with various discarded items arrayed outside she fantasized about the people behind their doors.

Room 452 displayed a pair of men's patent leather shoes and a pair of women's pumps in pink velvet. An empty wine bottle stood next to the shoes. (Prohibition had apparently not reached room service at The Breakers.) In this room, Violet decided, lived the film stars, Rudolph Valentino and Pola Negri, engaged in a secret tryst. (She might have been only twelve, but she read movie magazines and had at least a vague idea of what a tryst was.) He would be wrapped in a silk dressing gown and smoking an Egyptian cigarette in a long ivory holder, his dark hair slicked back, his eyebrows arched seductively. She, sheathed in a sheer pink negligee, would lie limply across the bed as if in a swoon.

Room 456 was nearly obstructed by an avalanche of newspapers, coffee cups, and a china plate filled with half smoked cigar butts. Violet was certain that behind that door was none other than Oliver "Daddy" Warbucks, wealthy munitions baron, who must be searching in vain for his Little Orphan Annie (personified by Violet herself). She, of course, would be as unaware of his presence as he would be of hers, and so the plucky little waif would wander off into unimaginable peril with only her devoted puppy, Sandy, for company. Violet's visualization of this fictional "Daddy" was tinged with an uncertain apprehension, a doubt about the state of affairs with her own daddy. But she was not yet able to form a clear picture in her mind to explain this perplexing anxiety.

At an intersection of hallways she picked a turning that brought her once again to a dead end. Here there was only one room, a cloistered solitary retreat in the darkened, untraveled corridor. What denizens would need the privacy this sanctum provided? What devious plots were being hatched behind the door of room 493? She spied several empty bottles which, if she had been astute in the arcane study of liquor containers she might have deduced were gin bottles which very probably had once been filled with the real thing.

She was about to retrace her steps when she noticed that the door to room 493 was slightly ajar. Gruff voices and the clanking of glassware drew her irresistibly toward the opening. She was now skirting the breach between fantasy and voyeurism. She saw four men seated around a table playing cards. A young woman in sequined flapper attire leaned against a big, bear-like man—a heavy set, heavily tanned, imposing figure with rolled shirt sleeves, open collar and bright red suspenders. Ah, Violet thought, mobsters and their moll! A sudden awareness came over her that she was witnessing something she wasn't supposed to see. It was the common quandary of growing up: it pushed and it pulled as you stood on the brink of discovery and the probable loss of innocence. Had she known how accurate her intuition had been she might have scurried away quite rapidly. Instead she watched and listened, intrigued, a bit guilty, but completely fascinated.

A dull grey haze of tobacco smoke hung above the men's heads. To the left of the man in the red suspenders sat a small, mousey man with a thin mustache. He had removed his jacket but kept on his neatly buttoned vest. An expertly knotted pale blue silk necktie was tucked into the top of his vest. For some reason, this swatch of blue intrigued Violet; it was like a ribbon given by a Princess to a jousting knight. The man with the red suspenders knocked a clenched fist against the table, turned to the man with the neatly buttoned vest and blue tie and said, "Check." This man ruffled the cards he was holding, grimaced, dropped them to the table and said, "I'm out."

Of the other two men, their backs turned toward her, Violet could construct no accurate image. One sat hunched over the table and wore a sleeveless undershirt. He seemed to be sweating a lot. The other was in a three piece suit and didn't sweat at all. This man pushed a stack of chips forward and as he leaned Violet caught a glimpse of a familiar figure: it was the piano man she had seen talking to Rose in the lobby!

"Big Bill," said the man in the neatly buttoned vest, "the boss needs you back in office."

The flapper girl whispered something in the ear of the man with

6

the red suspenders. He emitted a low chuckle, then he said, "Don't I know it! But you boys," he continued, "first have to settle your differences."

"That's up to Scarface and the Gennas, ain't that right?" The man with the neatly buttoned vest was looking at the piano man, a look, Violet decided, which would have been described as "daggers" in the popular literature.

The sweating man in the undershirt also looked at the piano man. He shook his head as if in warning.

"Why ask me?" said the piano man.

"Yer the big man these days, ain't ya?" said buttoned vest.

"Yeah, and you just switched loyalties out of the goodness of your heart."

"I just come over 'cause I like I-talian food."

"You better go back and tell Hymie and Bugs to cool it…or someone will cool it for them."

"Gentlemen, gentlemen," said the man with the red suspenders. Let's settle this later. Now we have a bet on the table. I'll see you and raise you a hundred."

Violet was getting a cramp in her leg as she stood, transfixed but afraid to move in case she'd be noticed by the men. Afraid, also, she might miss something…juicy. At last, prudence won over curiosity and she backed away cautiously, turned and ran at a pace the popular literature would have described as "lickety-split." Unfortunately she ran down a dead-end corridor. There was the usual low table with potted plant and a curtained window which overlooked the tennis court on this side of the building. She could see people swinging rackets below and the small white ball flying back and forth over the net. I should learn that game, she thought. She turned to retrace her steps back to the main corridor.

She bolted around a corner and collided with the man with the neatly buttoned vest and blue tie from room 493. "Watch where yer goin' ya little brat," snapped the man. He smelled like booze and after shave. That and the heavy odor of garlic, one of Violet's least favorite smells. Violet knew she should apologize to the man, but something prevented her from uttering anything. Perhaps it was the sense she had of something slightly sinister about this man's demeanor. He seemed no longer to be the knight carrying the Princess' blue ribbon of favor.

She was turned around by the collision. The maze of corridors was confusing enough without having just run smack into a man on whom she had been spying. She wandered aimlessly for a while, then she remembered the room numbers; all she needed to do was follow the numbers down to room 406, her own room. But somehow she was at another dead end. The same one with the potted plant and the window? She looked out of the window expecting to see the tennis court but she was apparently at the opposite end of that wing of the building. All she could see was an expanse of sand and a man walking across it. He was not wearing a swimming suit. Neither was the second man who was following him.

Back at the room, Violet approached her mother, gently touched her arm and asked, "Mummy, will Daddy be coming tomorrow?"

"No, Dear, he won't."

"The day after, then?"

Hazel Valentine closed the book she was reading to Rose and Gladys. "Dear, why don't you take your sisters down to the beach? Get your swimming suits on. I have some unpacking to do, and then I'll join you. After that we can have a nice dinner and watch the sunset."

"But Mummy, you didn't answer my question."

"Daddy isn't coming this time, Honey."

"But why would we go on vacation without him? It doesn't make any sense."

"We'll talk about this later. You run along and help your sisters on with their suits. That's a good girl."

# 2

## The Beach

When they descended the elevator and trooped through the lobby toward the exit that fronted on the beach, they were wearing their bathing suits and had towels draped over their shoulders. The desk clerk noticed the girls and immediately warned them that the breakers were too high to swim safety. "Just walk on the beach or sit on the sand," he said. "Tomorrow is another day." There's always another day, thought Violet, but she obeyed and they walked along the beach to where rocks were piled up and tufts of coarse grass poked through the sandy soil and waved in the breeze.

The children had reached a spot where heavy breakers rolled to shore and crashed against large boulders, sending up spectacular fans of spray against the azure sky. The boulders had been placed there to prevent the ocean from reclaiming the beach it had created so many millennia ago. Sea birds circled and dived along the nearby coral reef, reappearing above the waves with an anemone or a small octopus dangling from their beaks. The three girls sat on a large rock overlooking a tide pool where they hoped to sight a barracuda or a shark (or maybe even a whale) but saw only a small sea turtle flailing its stubby legs as it tried to return to the ocean. Violet decided to hurry the turtle along on its quest by pitching it into the surf but a gull swooped down and snatched it away.

The rough woolen material of her suit itched and Violet wished she were frolicking in the waves instead of sitting on a hard rock. She looked down the beach and saw a man shuffling hurriedly, kicking up little explosions of sand as he went. Why didn't he take his shoes off, Violet wondered? Then she recognized the familiar form of the piano man still in three piece suit and tie but looking disheveled and stressed. He seemed not to notice the three girls on the rocks by the tide pool and continued up the beach toward the hotel at a pace somewhat impractical for negotiating sand in dress shoes. Violet could see three sets of footprints which softened and filled when the surf rolled over them like a glaze. Curiously, two sets went down the beach but only one came back up.

The wind sounded its fury as it bombarded the beach goers. Gulls shrieked in high-pitched concert with the waves thundering against the rocks. Violet felt as if she were encased in a cocoon of pure sound. In the tide pool small hermit crabs were hiding in the shadows but now and then a gull swooped down and scooped one up in its bill. Other gulls chased it, attempting to steal its prize. In the end, whichever was the largest gull prevailed. Then the cycle of fish and chase and grab began again.

The younger girls were getting bored and began taunting each other the way siblings will do. Violet was annoyed at having to be the peacemaker; it taxed her creative energy to always have to invent new ways to intervene before things got out of hand. "Let's go write our names in the sand," she told Rose and Gladys, raising her voice to be heard above the wind which whined and whistled and threw spray up on the rocks.

They found sticks and went to work scribbling letters just at the edge of wet sand where the salt water receded leaving its own signature in curlicues of foam. Violet again noticed the sets of footprints still faintly apparent although the sea sucked away at them. She couldn't shake her curiosity about the two men who had made those marks and so she determined to investigate the matter. She would follow the disappearing trail.

She tried to tell Rose and Gladys to stay where they were but her voice was eaten by the gale. She used hand gestures and they nodded in acknowledgement. She hurried down the beach in the direction of the dissolving prints but the evidence of the men's passing faded as she reached the drier, wind-blown sand. A dead fish here, a piece of sea weed there, a hermit crab retreating into its shell, were scattered along the beach but the footprints were gone. She was at another dead end.

The faint traces of the footsteps had pointed her along a vector which she followed by instinct, like a cat sensing the evaporated trail of a mouse. Something compelled her to complete this haphazard reconnaissance across the sand and among the giant boulders. Curiosity, the popular literature might say, could kill the cat. She carried on quite cat-like toward a collection of boulders forming a sea wall where the breakers smashed relentlessly. The salt spray stung her eyes and coated her lips. She licked her lips nervously, wishing for something sweet to counter the acrid sensation. The first thing she saw as she reached the sea wall was a swatch of pale blue.

It was difficult deciphering the lumpy shape wedged between the grey rocks. Was it a discarded overcoat or part of some shipwreck dashed upon the shore by the ferocity of an angry sea? As she stared she slowly began to piece together certain familiar elements into a more recognizable whole. She discerned a pair of freshly shined shoes, a thin mustache on a doughy face striped with rivulets of crimson, a twisted hand rising up from the sorry heap as if clawing its way to the sky, and the ragged remnants of a blue necktie hanging from a pocket. Suddenly she knew. The body lying in the crevasse between two of the boulders was that of the man with the neatly buttoned vest (and pale blue tie) who Violet had seen playing cards and who she had bumped into in the hallway. He must have been one of the two men Violet had observed on the beach from her vantage point at the hallway window.

A person you'd never met, who you'd seen only fleetingly (and bumped into only briefly) and who you would never ever talk to unless properly introduced and even then would only recite the memorized niceties appropriate to a difference in age, station, and interests—that person shouldn't elicit pangs of grief or the shock of sudden loss. And this man who smelled of garlic and whiskey had frightened her—yes, she could admit that now. Nothing to be upset about. Yet as she stood, teetering on the slippery sea wall, an anguished wail issued from her lips which was lost in the loud thrashing of the breakers. As she stared in disbelief at the man she never had known, had never cared to know, she uttered, "Oh, Father!" Her utterance shocked her as much as the bizarre scene before her on the rocks. Father?

At once another notion entered her clever mind: the second man on the beach! The piano man! He had just been there. Was she a witness to a murder? Now she was intrigued. A sensation, an excitement, an exhilaration integral to the fantasy world of childhood intervened as if to protect her from reality in its harshness and brutality. This was a good as a cover of Weird Tales! (Not that Hazel Valentine would ever let her daughter read stories like "The Rats in the Walls" by H. P. Lovecraft or Poe's "Murders in the Rue Morgue," but pulps were passed around on the school yard and Violet was an avid reader of horror fiction.) It was better than a Lon Chaney movie! (It was enough that Violet had seen the marquee posters for "Phantom of the Opera" and "The Unholy Three"—of course she couldn't attend such cinema offerings…could she?) Wait 'til she showed her sisters…

But no, her sisters were too young to see this bloody mess that had once been a man. But Violet had to look. She moved closer. The man that had been ugly and crude in life was transformed by death into something beautiful, something which glistened bright red against the grey granite, something timeless, otherworldly, and beckoning. Violet examined the ragged opening on the fallen angel's forehead where a bullet had pierced his skull. White fragments of bone and the pulpy pink-grey of brain matter were visible as the ocean spray washed away the ruby-red blood.

The way the man was sprawled with arms and legs in impossible positions made Violet think of a marionette that had broken all its strings and fallen in a heap. The buttons of his once neatly buttoned vest had popped. The blue necktie, one end tucked into a pocket, was flapping in the wind, the only movement in this still life scene—still *death* scene. Still, death wasn't what Violet thought about as she surveyed the twisted form wedged so ignobly in the rocks as if regurgitated by the angry sea and deposited, cast-off, dumped, upchucked—just so much unwanted sea-drift. Violet wasn't thinking about death or briny offerings from Davy Jones' locker. She was thinking about the pale blue necktie.

When she returned to where her sisters were playing a game of tic-tac-toe in the wet sand, the sky had clouded to a dark grey and the gale had intensified to a howling blast. "Girls! We've got to go in," she cried. The impending mistral would bring heavy rain and a cyclonic windstorm to this tropical paradise of palms and sand— Violet could feel it in her bones. She had to pull Rose and Gladys forcefully from the beach. They entered the hotel to find their mother standing with arms folded and one foot tapping loudly on the tiled floor.

"I've been calling you for ages," said their mother.

"We couldn't hear you, Mummy. The wind was too loud," Violet answered, tears beginning to form in her eyes.

"It's all right now, Sweetheart. You're all inside and the storm hasn't hit yet. Come get dressed now."

The trip up the elevator seemed to Violet to last forever; her temporal sense had raced ahead of the actual passage of time and slowed her world to a crawl. Mother, Rose and Gladys stood still as three plaster birds in a gently rocking gilded cage. As the red indicator lights blinked on and off for the second floor, Violet could feel the rolled up necktie she had secreted under her swimming suit begin to slip. Her hand went to the slight lump it made and arrested its movement.

The cage jerked, a bell rang, the fourth floor light flashed on and Hazel reached to pull back the gate and push open the elevator door. Someone was standing in the hallway, waiting for the elevator. Violet let out a gasp when she saw the piano man in front of her. The man smiled, which made the scar above his eyebrow momentarily arch. He was smiling and looking at Rose for whom he had played "Yes, We Have No Bananas." Violet couldn't move. Hazel had to take her arm and pull her from the elevator.

"Hello there," the man said to Rose. Hazel ushered her children down the hall as quickly as she could. Time returned to normal for Violet. When she was back in their room and removed her swimming suit she discovered to her horror that the necktie was missing. It must have slipped out as they hurried back to the room. If it had fallen out while she was still in the elevator…

The dining room of The Breakers, an extravagance of crystal, brass, and velvet, was peopled with gourmands exhibiting what Henry James called "the hotel spirit." It was as if this edifice of luxury had taken on the role of educator by example; had elevated both the ordinary minions and their wealthy contemporaries (James would say, "their betters") to a state of recreational ecstasy; had enabled them to embrace this tropical Vanity Fair, this beacon of the Gilded Age, this perfumed replica of Xanadu as their well-deserved (albeit self-indulged) domicile away from home, emblematic of taste and refinement (which taste and refinement they were capable of renting by the day, week or month). In short, these gluttons were reveling in a sumptuous splendor which might dissipate during the return trip home but which, momentarily, suited their sense of privilege.

Hazel Valentine felt fortunate to be enjoying the service, the white linen, the silver settings and the candles. She was no glutton, did not have the arrogance of affluence to jade her or make her less appreciative of the excellence of the establishment—the professionalism and expertise that others in the dining room may have demanded or taken for granted. She just liked a good meal and was, at least for the time being, able to put the cost of it out of her mind. Her husband, Harry, would be incensed at her imprudent lavishness once he discovered she had ventured off to Florida with the children in tow. She was, at the moment, less concerned with Harry's inevitable anger than with the oyster cocktail in front of her.

Violet stared dubiously at her brimming bowl of green turtle soup, perhaps expecting a short nose and blinkless eyes to poke up suddenly from the grimy looking concoction. She had requested the soup because of a sort of perverse curiosity, but now was regretting her impulsiveness. Her sisters were enjoying roasted almonds and sweet mustard pickles—they were less adventurous than she. There was a Waldorf salad and warm bread and butter on the way, so Violet stirred her soup absentmindedly and surveyed the room for anything of interest.

She spotted the big man from the poker game seated at a table by the window, accompanied by a woman in a dark silk dress and a necklace of pearls that glowed in the candle light as if they were lit from within. The arched window behind them looked out over the rambling covered promenade which was currently being pelted by sheets of rain. Too bad the tempest prevented them from dining alfresco on the veranda or in the courtyard under the palms. Maybe the storm would pass by tomorrow.

What to order...roast stuffed squab (freshly killed) with wild grape sauce, and potatoes Yvette with fresh mushrooms in cream? Or fillet of bass in sauce, or Welsh rarebit with bacon, or braised sweetbreads with mushrooms...no, that last one sounded worse than the turtle soup. Ah...chicken à la king would hit the spot! Maybe some banana fritters with that. Mother, of course, ordered the roast ribs of prime beef with potatoes au gratin and broccoli in Hollandaise. Rose and Gladys allowed Mother to order for them:

roast chicken and mashed potatoes. And dessert, of course, but what? Meringue glaze or lemon chiffon pie, caramel custard pudding or butter pecan ice cream? Decisions, decisions, decisions.

The man and woman at the table by the window were William Hale "Big Bill" Thompson and his wife, Mary, also known as Maysie. Big Bill was over six feet tall and weighed in at over 300 pounds. Thompson had been mayor of Chicago from 1915 to 1923 and was now eyeing the 1927 race. His father, William Senior, had been a real estate developer in Chicago, building a fortune after the Great Chicago Fire as his holdings, close to downtown, had not turned to ashes as had most of the city center. Bill Junior, possibly spoiled by his family wealth, spurned college for a career as a cow poke in Wyoming and New Mexico. He returned to Chicago sporting a ten gallon hat, took over the business and ran for Alderman on the South Side in a ward that was fast becoming notorious as a red light district. It was called the Levee.

As Alderman of the Second Ward, Thompson came under the influence of two gangsters known as the Lords of the Levee, Michael "Hinky Dink" Kenna and John J. "Bathhouse" Coughlin. Hinky Dink and Bathhouse ran protection rackets in the neighboring First Ward, the "Old Levee," and sought to expand their operations into Thompson's. Brothels and gambling dens and dives such as the Everleigh Club ran unchecked during Thompson's tenure in the "New Levee."

By 1915, Big Bill was Mayor of Chicago, having beaten out a Democrat, a Socialist, a Progressive and a Prohibitionist (with support from the Lords of the Levee) to become the city's first and last Republican mayor. He supported Blacks and Women's Sufferage but waffled on many issues such as Prohibition and the Teachers' Union. He was flamboyant and theatrical. He once rode a horse into the council chambers, and on another occasion, staged a political debate with two white rats standing in for his opponents. During World War I he was pro-German, a stance which garnered him the nickname, "Kaiser Bill." He was anti-British and threatened to punch King George in the snoot if he ever met him. This did little to advance his popularity.

His unique personality failed to get him re-elected in 1923. There were just too many scandals. A race-riot in 1919 showed him up as inept when he failed to act promptly. There were rumors that the Germans had used Thompson's political speeches as propaganda during the war. In his third race for mayor he was badly beaten by William Dever, a reformer.

In order to keep his name before the public, he staged an expedition to the South Seas in search of a tree-climbing fish—this species of fish, he claimed, could come out of the water and live on land, could jump three feet into the air to catch grasshoppers, and could actually climb trees. The expedition got as far as New Orleans but Big Bill only got as far as Florida.

And so here he was with his wife, Maysie, who had once been a secretary in Big Bill's father's office. Big Bill's mother had objected to her son romancing the help, so the young couple eloped to Michigan. Maysie supported her husband's political ambitions, took pride in his successes and commiserated with him when he failed. She looked the other way when Bill entertained his female friends and was content with shopping and minor society events. They had reached a status quo in their relationship which was overdue for disintegration. There would be trouble in paradise.

Violet was shoveling a forkful of lemon chiffon pie into her mouth. She was disappointed that the restaurant didn't have key lime pie on the menu; she'd never tried the local delicacy, but had read in the fan magazines that movie stars savored the tart pie on their own visits to Palm Beach. Still, the lemon pie was delicious, a sweet ending to a bitter-sweet day. She still hadn't mentioned the dead body to her mother. She imagined it being carried out to sea by the storm, maybe eaten by a shark or a whale or a giant octopus. Then she imagined the man's ghost haunting the beach at night, looking for his killer—or for the young girl who neglected to report his demise.

Her attention wandered to the big man and his wife at the table by the window. Was he a gangster, she wondered? Was he planning to bump off the dark-skinned bus boy who was clearing the table? Darkies, she had heard them called. Darkies who had helped build the hotel and the neighboring town of West Palm Beach. Darkies who had been occupants of the neighboring shanty town called The Styx, a slum with no running water or sewage disposal, an eyesore that offended the white movers-and-shakers of Palm Beach, a horrid place of shacks and tents that disappeared in the flames of urban renewal—or so the legend said. Henry Morrison Flagler, owner and builder of The Breakers and the Royal Poinciana, the Florida East Coast Railroad, the Palm Beach Country Club and other venues, the great oil baron and real estate magnate, was said to have issued free tickets to a carnival to all his Black employees—an then ordered his henchmen to burn the Styx to the ground!

But now as Violet spied on Big Bill and his wife, a man approached and began whispering something in Big Bill's ear. He was gesturing in her direction. Big Bill was nodding. She recognized the piano man and a shiver went up her spine. Was that a fragment of blue protruding from the piano man's pocket? Was he showing this to the big man? Should she be afraid…really afraid?

Byron Grush

# 3

## The Casino

The following morning the ocean was still too choppy for swimming so the Valentines strolled a few yards south of the hotel to The Breaker's Casino, a luxurious bath house featuring a ten-foot deep salt-water pool, a diving tower and 1,000 dressing rooms. It was a two-story, colonial style building with a large courtyard in which the open-air pool was placed. On the surrounding pink Spanish tiles were set wooden deck chairs and tables where patrons could enjoy coffee or soft drinks. A railed second-floor observation deck ran around the perimeter of the interior space. Some came to swim, some to observe; professional diver, E. B. Jennison had been known to do hand stands on the Casino roof before flipping off into the water.

Rose Valentine had made a new friend at the pool: a girl her own age named Patricia. Patricia amazed Rose with stories about the playhouse her father had built for her back home in Hastings-on-Hudson, New York. It was two stories tall and had a kitchen with an electric stove on which Patricia could make cookies. It looked like Mount Vernon, George Washington's home, because Patricia's father had gotten a false front constructed for the movie set of the Marion Davies movie, "Little Old New York," and expanded it into a playhouse for his daughter. Her father, Patricia said, knew many movie stars. His name was Florenz Ziegfeld, Jr.

Did she have a pet dog, Rose wanted to know? Oh yes, she had 15 dogs, some canaries, a parrot, a cockatoo, rabbits, and several ponies. For her sixth birthday, her father had brought home a baby elephant which stayed on the property for the summer until it rejoined the Ringling Brother's Circus at winter quarters in Sarasota, Florida. In fact the family home, called Burkeley Crest, harbored many an exotic animal including two lion cubs, a tiger, two bears and a herd of deer. Flo Ziegfeld was planning on acquiring a pair of buffalo next.

Rose knew very little about the famous Broadway producer known as "Ziggy" to his friends. Violet, however, could recite significant facts about the King of Broadway and his Follies that she had gleaned from movie magazines. She knew, for instance, that little Patricia's parents were often engaged in the vicious cycle of spat and make-up, spat and make-up, spat and make-up. Violet was certain that both parents were not present at The Breakers. She had only seen Patricia's mother, former silent screen star, Billie Burke. It was probable that if Ziggy were here, he was at Bradley's gambling, but in fact he was in New York City, working on a new show.

Billie Burke had been as popular as Mary Pickford or Lillian Gish, starring in over 16 features and serials between 1916 and 1921. She was the daughter of the famous circus clown and performer, William Burke, and no stranger to the theatrical life. Hers had begun in 1903 on the London stage and had soon continued on Broadway, then in the movies. Even after her success in Hollywood, she decided to return to the stage in 1919 and would not make movies again until the financial crash of 1929 (which would wipe out most of her husband's fortune). She had met and married Florenz Ziegfeld in 1914. Together they built the fabulous mansion at Burkeley Crest (Billie and her mother owned the property). They set out to spoil their daughter Patricia rotten—but Patty remained sweet in spite of all her advantages.

Billie put her own money into Ziggy's productions, helping him through the ups and downs of his career. She never performed in any of the Follies—she was, she said, a *legitimate* stage actress. She put up with the parade of chorus girls that surrounded Flo but was incensed by the nude painting of Follies star Olive Thomas which he hung in his office. Thomas was married to Mary Pickford's brother Jack and died mysteriously of poisoning in a hotel room in Paris. Some say she had ingested Jack's mercury bichloride, a remedy for syphilis.

Patricia's mother was now sitting at a poolside table, dressed immaculately as usual in couture by Lucile. She was overly sensitive about her age (41) and rarely appeared publically in bathing clothes. At home she would dress in exercise tights and bloomers and she took boxing lessons with Ziggy, but Palm Beach was for maintaining a high-society image—Billie was an expert at that. When Violet approached asking for an autograph, Billie was gracious even though it was obvious that the Valentine family was not part of the social elite.

"Have you seen any of my films, sweetheart?" Billie asked Violet.

"Oh, no, Ma'am. Mother doesn't let me go to the cinema unless it is 'Alice in Cartoonland.' But I read all the fan magazines...oh, don't mention that to Mother, will you?"

Billie thought about some of her films: "The Frisky Mrs. Johnson," "Wanted: A Husband," "The Make-Believe Wife," and "The Education of Elizabeth." She told Violet, "It's just as well, Dear. Just as well you don't go to the cinema. Wait until you're older and then go to the theater. That's where the real art is."

"The magazines say you don't make movies any more because you're married. Is that true?"

"Precocious, aren't you, sweetie? I once thought that when an actress married she should leave the stage to take care of her husband. But I now I think there is no reason why marriage should necessarily compel an actress to forego her career. You can quote me on that last one."

"Did you bring your pet cheetahs along with you?"

"Dear heart, you read too many fan magazines! You should read books...good literature...appropriate for your age. When I was in England I knew Jim Barrie. He wrote the novel, *Peter and Wendy*. I wanted to be in that play *The Boy Who Wouldn't Grow Up*, but I was too old to play Wendy and I certainly didn't want to play the mother. Well, you know, age only matters if you're a cheese. Did you ever read *Peter Pan?*"

"My favorite books," Violet replied, "are the Oz books. *The Wonderful Wizard of Oz* is my favorite. That's the first one, with Dorothy and the scarecrow and the tin man and the lion. And the wicked witch!"

"Isn't there a good witch in it too?"

"Yes, but I liked the evil one better."

While Violet chattered away, no doubt boring Billie Burke to death, Rose and Patty were jumping into the pool repeatedly, trying to outdo each other in making the biggest splash. Gladys was coaxing her mother into the pool at the shallow end; she was still learning to swim. The storm that had battered the peninsula the previous day had dissipated so now the ever-glorious Florida sunshine caressed the land with the promise of blossoms and bulbous fruits. The ever-present gulls circled above the casino, vociferous with staccato cackling. Above the pool on the observation deck a lone figure lurked. His immaculate suit and vest seemed out of place, unnecessarily cumbersome, and definitely much too warm for the weather. But he was more happy being dapper than comfortable. He studied the scene below him, especially the trio of sisters he had passed in the hallway by the elevator—when he had found the pale blue necktie.

Violet had just finished relating the entire plot of *Tik-Tok of Oz*, about Betsy Bobbin and the Shaggy Man and the Nome King. Billie Burke was beginning to doze off. The warmth of the Florida sun was defeating her struggle to keep her eyes open. Violet's mother, wrapped in a red and white striped towel and dripping salt water suddenly appeared saying:

"Violet, don't bother the lady. Come along now and keep your sisters entertained."

"She isn't bothering me. She's been delightful. Telling me all about Oz," Billie said to Hazel Valentine. Thank you, Lord, for sending me this angel of a mother to rescue me from Nome Kings and Tik-Toks, she said to herself.

But after Hazel led the girl away, Billie's eyes finally closed. The world that had been one of brilliant Technicolor faded into sepia as the memory, so many years ago, of a marriage proposal by the dashing Enrico Caruso, played across her sleepy sensibilities like an old movie. Her suitors had been many, including Samuel Clemens who had been nearly fifty years her senior but handsome in a rugged, down-home way. However, it had been Florenz Ziegfeld who had swept her off her feet. Flo…the King of Broadway, the purveyor of extravagance, the object of every chorus girl's desire. How many sequined cuties surrounded him at this very moment?

Although the storm had passed, the wind still came in random gusts, like the coughing of an old man with bronchitis. Pennants on the Casino's roof flapped; beach umbrellas over the tables by the pool rippled and threatened to take flight. Violet pouted, being relegated to helping Gladys in and out of the shallow end; she was feeling sorry for herself of course, but at the same time, a smidgeon of guilt about neglecting to report what she perceived as a horrendous murder crept into her thoughts. She should at least tell Mother—but it was getting later and later to do so. Why hadn't the body been discovered? Hadn't the man been missed? If she didn't tell…would she be arrested as an accomplice? Spend the rest of her life in jail?

At the other end of the Casino, the piano man, as Violet had come to call him in her own mind, was talking to Rose and Patty, squatting precariously at the pool's edge. Violet frowned. At that moment she made the decision to tell her mother what she knew…or thought she knew. Grabbing Gladys by the hand she pulled her sibling along with her as she walked to the table where Hazel Valentine was in a conversation with another woman.

"Mother…"

"Don't bother me, dear, when I'm talking to someone. Run along and play with your sister," said Hazel.

"Aw..."

The woman was Mrs. E. F. Hutton, also known as Marjorie Merriweather Post. Besides being married to the wealthy financier, Marjorie was herself stinking rich, being the heiress and owner of the Postum Cereal Company of Battle Creek, Michigan, and an astute businesswoman who had parlayed her father's company into one of the most successful enterprises of the century. She was possibly the wealthiest woman in America and was worth at least $250 million dollars.

The Huttons had a house at Palm Beach in addition to a rustic retreat in the Adirondacks (the "rustic" Camp Topridge consisted of a main lodge and guest cabins totally almost 70 buildings on 300 acres) and a 54-room apartment in New York City. But the house at Palm Beach had proved too small for the lavish entertaining Marjorie liked to do. So Marjorie had commissioned Joseph Urban and Marion Sims Wyeth to design Mar-A-Lago on 17 acres of Palm Beach. Urban, an Austrian-American architect, had executed designs for William Randolph Hearst, the Metropolitan Opera, and Florenz Ziegfeld. Wyeth was a prominent Florida architect in his own right.

Marjorie was at her Palm Beach home while she oversaw

construction of the elaborate Spanish Colonial Revival style estate she would call Mar-A-Lago. E. F. Hutton, her most recent husband, maintained a branch of his brokerage firm in an office at The Breakers, just off the front porch, so Marjorie often visited friends at the hotel. She was now at the Casino to meet with Billie Burke, but seeing that her old friend was dozing, had elected instead to chat with Hazel Valentine, a fresh face here at Palm Beach and someone who would not require the kind of social posturing that put stress into one's leisure time. She was telling this rather common-place woman all about her latest discovery: a man named Clarence Birdseye who had developed a method of fast-freezing fruits and vegetables. She was thinking, she said, of purchasing the man's company and expanding Postum into something she would then call General Foods. Her own daughter, two year-old Deenie, was at home in New York with her mother-in-law, and Marjorie was just bored enough to open up to a total stranger.

While Hazel was elated to be trading small talk with this powerful woman, Violet could have cared less about the woman's wealth and status, but she had to admit to being fascinated by Mrs. Hutton's striking beauty and poise. Not to mention the sparkling diamond ring on her finger or the cascade of precious gems dangling around her neck. Gladys was tugging on her arm.

"But, Mother…"

"Off you go, Violet!"

Marjorie Merryweather Post Close Hutton, who was called "Maggie" by her close friends (and who had extended this consideration now to Hazel Valentine), smiled sweetly at Violet and watched as the two girls left to join Rose and Patty. Billie Burke was by this time snoring ungraciously, so Maggie continued describing her plans for Mar-A-Lago. The name was Spanish for "Between the Sea and the Lake," appropriate as the estate sprawled majestically between Lake Worth and the Atlantic Ocean.

When completed, Mar-A-Lago would be the fifth largest private residence in the country with 118 rooms, including 58 bedrooms, 33 bathrooms, and 12 fireplaces. It would have a 34 foot tall gold-leafed ceiling in the living room, marble floors, imported Spanish tiles throughout and a 75 foot tower rising high above Ocean Boulevard. There would be royal palms and citrus groves, a nine-hole golf course, guest houses, a swimming pool and private beach. It would cost over 8 million dollars.

"Are you going to the Saint Patrick's Day Ball?" Maggie asked.

"Oh...I don't know. I haven't a gown," Hazel answered, a bit embarrassed.

"There are some lovely shops at the other hotel...the Royal Poinciana. I'm sure you could find something...adequate."

Hazel had yet to experience the long hallways and covered porches of the Poinciana—hallways so long that messenger boys rode bicycles to deliver letters. The shops were numerous and diversified: millinery, jewelry, gifts and gimcracks, and all manner of sweets, cosmetics, toys and sundries to edify any boarder's needs and desires—and all at a price that reminded one of the prestige of affording to recreate at Palm Beach's spectacular hotel venues.

"I'll be certain to investigate the shops," Hazel replied. The Saint Patrick's Day Ball! Hazel did so want to attend. If only Harry...

"I think Billie is stirring over there. I really must go talk to her. It's been great fun chatting with you, Hazel. I hope we can get together again sometime. Don't forget about the Ball!"

The piano man had disappeared by the time Violet and Gladys reached Rose at the other end of the pool. Patty had returned to her own mother, possibly to greet her mother's friend Maggie Hutton, or possibly to annoyingly interject herself into a conversation where she would be better seen than heard. Violet immediately quizzed Rose:

"What were you talking about with the piano man?"

"The piano man? Oh, you mean Mr. Jones? That's his name, stupid."

"You shouldn't talk to strangers, you know. And don't call me 'stupid.' What did you talk about?"

"Oh...he just asked if we had enjoyed the beach the other day. He wanted to know if we had found anything."

"Found anything? Like what?"

"Oh, you know...sea shells or that sort of thing."

"I don't want you talking to him again, Rose. I'll tell Mother and she'll command you not to talk to him."

"Honestly, Vi, I don't see what you're so mad about. He's a nice man. He said he would play more songs for me on the piano."

"I'm going to tell Mother."

But tell her what, Violet thought to herself? Tell her I think he's a murderer and there's a body down on the beach? And I'm just now telling about it? Maybe it would be better to start with just one thing at a time. The body. Tell her about the body. She would wait until she and Mother were alone, once they got back to the room. Then she'd tell.

*   *   *

It was possible, if you so desired, to travel all the way from New York City to Havana, Cuba, on the Havana Special, another of Henry Morrison Flagler's enterprises. It was 1,523 miles to Key West, Florida, by train along the Florida East Coast Railroad and its northern affiliates, and another 1,596 miles to Cuba by steamboat. The trip lasted 42 hours. The train consisted of Pullman coaches, six sleepers, a dining car, a lounge car, and an observation car. The lounge car had separate areas for men and women, including baths and was serviced by what the railroad termed "a trained Filipino attendant."

Harry Valentine wasn't going all the way to Cuba. His destination was Palm Beach where his wife and daughters had gone, needing, Hazel had said in the brief note she had left, some personal time apart from him. The train, Number 141, was pulled by engine Number 10701C, a heavyweight Pacific-type oil-burning steam locomotive with a 4-6-2 wheel arrangement. It left New York's Pennsylvania Station at 10:05 PM and rolled through Newark, Trenton, West Philadelphia, Baltimore, and Washington to arrive at Richmond, Virginia, by the next morning, a distance of 340 rail miles. West Palm Beach was at milepost 1300. The train used the Pennsylvania Railroad's tracks to Washington, the Richmond, Fredericksburg & Potomac tracks to Richmond, and the Atlantic Coast Line tracks to Jacksonville where it picked up Flagler's Florida East Coast line.

Harry was stiff from sleeping sitting up in the Pullman car. He yawned and stretched as the porter came down the aisle announcing breakfast. His chief worry, beside that of reuniting (with minimal strife) with his family, was leaving his bookstore at 151 Pierrepont Street closed and unattended; his only employee, Theodora Adams, had walked out on him after the confrontation with Hazel.

Theo had been insulted by Hazel's contention that she was leading Harry astray and hurt by Harry's denial to Hazel of their clandestine affaire de Coeur. Their tryst of the previous afternoon, the one Hazel had interrupted, was evidence enough for Theo of Harry's feelings for her. Indeed, she believed the bookseller was on the verge of separation from that grousing queen bee, that despotic ball-buster of a whining, conniving, controlling spouse. Harry, apparently, didn't see Hazel in that light. His fling with Theo was simply that: a brief indiscretion. A foolhardiness.

The bookstore was Harry's passion, not Theo, nor for that matter, Hazel. He squirreled himself away there day after day waiting for the occasional customer to spot the innocuous looking shop on the first floor of the brownstone where the Valentines made their home—a home that Hazel loathed. Much too close to the unwholesome port area of Red Hook she said. Harry, on the other hand, loved the neighborhood, the block houses, the very smell of history, the old church, the mix of immigrants both old and young…it was exciting.

Valentine's Rare Books and Circulation Library also attracted local authors. A young man in his early twenties named Frank Belknap Long frequented the bookstore, rummaging for antique tomes. He wanted to be a writer, he said. One day he brought with him a tall, gaunt man who looked like he had slept at the narrow end of the Flatiron building. The man lived, he said, about four blocks south on Clinton Street. He was maybe ten years the senior to Long, and Long obviously looked up to him. His name was Howard Philip Lovecraft, he was a writer, and he was working on a story about Red Hook and Flatbush, about the area's squalid underbelly.

Lovecraft described for Harry his notion of the place: its sounds of "the lapping oily waves at its grimy piers and the monstrous organ litanies of the harbor whistles." He talked of the "processions of blear-eyed and pockmarked young men" that fascinated and chilled him and were suggestive of "primitive half-ape savagery" which made him believe that hidden there among the decay of worn stoops and rusted gates was something…evil. A horror born from the primordial—a horror certain denizens of the district worshiped with cult-like rituals.

Harry shook it all off, not sharing Lovecraft's macabre vision of the harbor at Red Hook. His was more romantic: he envisioned a gnarly old sea salt strutting around a widow's walk on the copula of a hundred year-old house on the hill, gazing through his spy glass at the tall ships in the harbor; horse-drawn carriages clattering through the narrow streets conveying men and women in formal attire—beaver-skin hats and silk cravats for the men, wide-brimmed, many-flowered hats and morning dresses with puffy ham-sleeves for the women. Brooklyn evoked for Harry a pseudo-nostalgia for a bygone era he had never known…but which he was more comfortable in than his own.

He enjoyed the company of the young authors and soon a group of them began meeting at the bookstore. The Kalem Club, as it was called, revolved around Lovecraft who, as a successful writer of fantasy, was their dean, mentor and chief inspiration. All of members' surnames began with "K," "L," or "M," hence the club was called "Kalem." Harry didn't manage to sell many books because of this literary circle, but he felt immersed in a contemporary cultural movement, albeit one that was born from the popular literature of pulp-fiction fantasy and horror.

The train rattled on. Harry Valentine rubbed the sleep from his eyes and hurried down the rocking corridor to the dining car where he would partake of a breakfast featuring fresh citrus, a prelude to the tropical paradise of the Sunshine State.

# 4

## The Jungle

Besides bathing at the Casino swimming pool or in the ocean, there wasn't much to do in Palm Beach. There were the shops, the afternoon teas and occasional concerts at the Royal Poinciana's Cocoanut Grove, the tennis courts and the golf links—ordinary faire for the rich and famous and not so very exciting. One ventured out in search of adventure once one got bored, which was often. The grounds and gardens around the hotels were beautiful, of course; one could stroll all day down palm-lined walk-ways. But the more exotic sights were far afield and the requisite mode of transportation, the way to really get around, was by Africo-mobile.

All the hotels offered a fleet of human-powered carts: comfortable wicker chairs for one or two on wheels, and connected to a bicycle-like device upon which sat a uniformed Black man with the insignia of his hotel on his cap, who pedaled guests down the Jungle Trail beneath the coconut palms to a densely vegetated area called "The Jungle." Once at The Jungle the carts followed a serpentine pathway that transported visitors to a wild, exotic land.

There were always possible side trips to the Ostrich Farm, the Alligator Farm (where Alligator Joe had wrestled alligators for sport…and an entrance fee…daily at 3:30 PM, up until his death in 1915), the Big Maddock and Matthams Pineapple Grove, Charles and

Frances Cragin's Reve d'Ete or "Dream of Summer" (a 35 acre botanical garden some called the "Garden of Eden"), the Florida Gun Club which featured live bird shoots, or of course, fishing from The Breaker's pier. But The Jungle…The Jungle was where one could marvel at the convoluted shapes of ancient banyan trees and snake along narrow passageways where the twisted roots and branches of mangroves formed an intricate mesh seemingly impossible to penetrate. At points the path was so narrow through the mangroves and the canopy so low that the wheeled chairs were pushed instead of peddled to avoid becoming snagged.

There were rubber trees, saw palmettos with their fan-shaped fronds, Bismarck palms with their interweaved bark looking like tall, cylinder-shaped baskets, and banyan trees grown from seeds deposited by birds in the crowns of palm trees, with roots which dripped like stalactites reaching for the ground. The banyan enveloped and killed the palm and spread into a massive, impossibly complex structure which forever fascinated people. It was often called "the strangler fig."

In India, the banyan tree was sacred, a symbol of eternal life. The baby Krishna lay snuggled in a banyan leaf; Shiva sat quietly under the banyan with rishis at his feet. In the Philippines, banyan trees were thought to harbor evil spirits; children were warned away from them. In Guam, the tree was believed to be the realm of fairies and goblins and the Taotaomona, their prehistoric ancestors. In Hong Kong, Buddhists tied joss paper prayers onto oranges and flung them up into the tree for good luck. This very same year at his home in

Fort Meyers, Florida, Thomas Edison imported a four-foot tall banyan tree to explore using its sap to produce natural rubber. Henry Ford and Harvey Firestone would visit the inventor's winter home with great expectations. They would be disappointed.

The Jungle consisted mostly of red mangroves, called "walking trees" because of their tangled prop roots. The trees were ideally suited for the Florida climate and soil. They were able to extract fresh water from salt and they provided nesting areas for pelicans and spoonbills. They occurred in abundance at the water's edge. The mangrove forest in The Jungle was old-growth in salty soil through which the wheelchair path had been carved into serpentine "S" curves, creating the experience of traveling through a maze, and of being caught in a web of spidery forms, once writhing, now frozen and eerily still. Only the wind whistling through the dense matrix of roots and branches gave a sense of animation to the mangrove forest.

The wicker chair was designed for two adults but the four Valentines squeezed into it by having little Gladys sit on her mother's lap while Violet and Rose crunched together on the other side of the seat. There was the inevitable squirming and poking as the "Palm Beach Cab" traversed the hard-packed trail. Their chair was part of a caravan of three such vehicles and Violet could hear the "Oohs" and "Ahs" of the other passengers as they passed unfamiliar and exotic plants.

"Mother," whined Rose, "why can't we go to the beach? This is boring!"

"Hush, Rose," answered Hazel Valentine. "This is educational."

"Mother," Rose insisted, "please tell the Darkey to take us back!"

"Rose! Do not call the man a 'Darkey.' He is a Negro and I'm sure he is a very nice man. Hush up and enjoy the sights."

The "Darkey" was in fact a very nice man whose name was Benjamin Pope. Pope had first come to The Breakers in 1916, attracted by the prospect of watching a baseball game between the Lincoln Giants and the Indianapolis ABCs. The Breakers and the Royal Poinciana hotels had hired the two teams for an exhibition game that winter, each sponsoring a rival team. Both were all-Negro teams who played in the days before the advent of the Negro League. The Giants' shortstop was John Henry Lloyd and their pitcher was Cyclone Joe Williams. The ABCs' second baseman was Bingo DeMoses and their pitcher was Dizzy Dismukes.

Growing up as a teenager in Jacksonville, Florida, Ben Pope had idolized these great athletes, but opportunities to see Black teams play rarely arose. Jim Crow laws kept Blacks off white baseball teams, so exhibition games were the only possibilities for Blacks to play publically. And the only way Benjamin Pope could get in to see the game was as an employee of one of the hotels. For Pope, working at one of the Flagler hotels was a far better prospect than rolling cigars or picking grapefruit. Since most of the tourists were from the North, there were few incidents of racist treatment by hotel guests. So he stayed on and gradually worked his way up to peddle-cab driver.

And Jim Crow was still alive and well in Florida. Only two years ago, in the tiny hamlet of Rosewood, there had been a lynching and a massacre which had destroyed the Black community by fire and murder. A white woman, Fanny Taylor, claimed to have been raped by a Black man. It happened that a Ku Klux Klan rally was being held in the nearby town of Gainesville. A man named Jesse Hunter had recently escaped from a Black chain gang and so suspicion fell on him as the assailant. Taylor's husband, James, appealed to the Klansmen to avenge his wife.

Accounts of incident tell of a posse of four to five hundred men combing the woods around the Taylor home. The posse became a mob. A man named Sam Carter was accused of harboring Hunter. He was tortured, shot, and hung from a tree. In another incident the mob approached a house where they hoped to find a friend of Carter's name Sylvester Carrier. They shot his dog. When his mother came to the door they shot her. They burned the house. Some of the Black residents who hadn't fled into the swamps fought back. In the end, at least six Blacks and two whites were dead, animals were slaughtered and buildings burned to the ground. The town was deserted and was never repopulated.

As the wheeled chair wound through the mangrove forest, Ben Pope began to sing an old folk song from the Bahamas about a woman who drank too much:

*Mama don't want no peas an' rice an' coconut oil,*
*Mama don't want no peas an' rice an' coconut oil,*
*Mama don't want no peas an' rice,*
*Mama don't want no coconut oil,*
*Just a bottle of brandy handy all the day!*

The trio of Africo-mobiles rounded a curve and came to stop. Before them, blocking the narrow path was another wheeled wicker chair which lay on its side. A stout woman was struggling to reattach a wheel that had come off. Her wide-brimmed hat lay in the dust. The driver was nowhere to be seen. The Valentine's chair was in the lead so Ben Pope hopped off his saddle and came to the woman's aid. He attempted to take the wheel from her but she reared back suddenly.

"I got it okay. Just hand me that nut over there will ya?" said the woman.

"Please let me hep yo, Ma'am."

"Well, you steady it while I fasten the nut to the axle. I *am* capable of doing it myself, however. Just so you know."

"Yes, Ma'am. I see you is."

And so it went. Finally, the cart was upright and the woman shook the dust and dirt from her dress. The driver had apparently panicked when the wheel had come off and had run away. Not to be defeated by the situation, the woman hitched up her skirts and mounted the saddle, preparing to drive the vehicle back to the hotel herself.

"I tell ya," she said to no one in particular, "life is just one disaster after another!"

Once the woman had peddled out of earshot, Ben Pope offered his own unique observation saying, "I's been here ten year, an' I ain't never seen nothin' like that befo'. That is some high-powered lady, that's fo' sure!"

Hazel had no idea who this strange woman was but Violet had recognized her from a picture in one of the magazines she read so clandestinely. In the picture the woman was younger, standing majestically tall and proud in a long flowing gown and flowered hat that denoted an earlier era. Violet remembered every word of the article: this surely must be she—the Heroine of the Titantic, the Unsinkable Mrs. Brown.

Margaret Tobin had been born in Hannibal, Missouri, some thirty years later than that small town's other famous resident, Samuel Clemens, aka Mark Twain. Her father had been an abolitionist and had worked with the Underground Railroad, a dangerous thing to do in Missouri before the Emancipation Proclamation. At thirteen she left school and worked at a factory striping tobacco leaves. She would later study with a tutor and attend the Carnegie Institute in New York as one of its first female students.

As a young woman she had moved to Leadville, Colorado, in hopes of marrying a rich man but instead fell in love with James Joseph Brown, an Irish immigrant who had little more to his name than she had. But there was apparently something called the "Brown luck." J. J. hit a seam of ore at the Little Johnny Mine where he worked as superintendant and was rewarded by his employers with 12,500 shares of stock and a seat on the board of the Ibex Mining Company. By 1894 the Browns had a $30,000 Victorian mansion in Denver. Three years later they built a summer home in nearby Bear Creek and began building social connections.

Margaret had worked in the soup kitchens in Leadville and had been involved in the Women's Suffrage Association. Now in Denver she helped found the Denver Woman's Club, raised funds for the building of a Catholic church and hospital and worked to establish the first juvenile court system in the United States. She ran for a U. S. Senate seat eight years before women had the vote but withdrew from the race at her husband's insistence. They divorced in 1909; with the settlement, Margaret Brown was a wealthy woman.

The Browns had two children who they sent to Europe for their education. Margaret also traveled extensively and was fluid in several languages. The popular plays and movies that would be made about her life many years later characterized her as an uneducated, social climbing, hillbilly sort of woman—the opposite was true. She would become known as "The Unsinkable Molly Brown" although she was never called Molly. it was easier to sing "Molly" than "Margaret," hence the Hollywood version. She was Maggie to her friends.

In 1912 she and her daughter, Helen, now on a break from her studies at the Sorbonne, had been traveling in Europe. Recently they had visited John Astor and his new wife in Cairo, Egypt. In London, Margaret received an urgent message that her grandson, Lawrence, was seriously ill back in the States. Leaving Helen in London, Margaret traveled to Cherbourg, France, where she boarded the first available ocean liner headed to American: the Titanic.

It was a dark and stormy night…no, not really; it was a calm and clear and moonless night. They were four days out into the middle of the North Atlantic. The telegraphed iceberg warnings lay buried in a stack of other messages. The captain had elected not to steer south to avoid icebergs; he believed they were clear of them. But lookouts sighted a huge iceberg dead ahead and notified the bridge. The engines were reversed and the gigantic ship swerved, barely escaping a collision, but she grazed an underwater outcropping of the iceberg ever so slightly. Just slightly enough to tear a long gash along her side.

It was about 11:30 at night and Margaret Brown was curled up on her brass bed reading a book by lamp light. She felt a crash and was thrown from the bed. Quickly she hurried from her stateroom to discover what had happened and encountered men on the gangway in their pajamas, complaining about the cold and about having to leave their smoking-rooms. Nothing seemed amiss, so Maggie returned to her stateroom and resumed reading.

Soon she heard the people in the next stateroom talking. "We should go on deck to see what has happened," someone said. Again she arose and peered into the corridor outside of her room where she saw six or seven stewards and one officer forcing an auger through a hole in the floor. This bizarre sight further perplexed her as she perceived the action was taking place with a great deal of levity on the part of the crew. What ever can have happened, she wondered?

After a short while she saw her curtains moving and again looked out. There, staring back at her was a man with a blanched face and protruding eyes looking as if he were haunted. He gasped for breath and uttered, "Get your life-saver!"

Five of the Titanic's water-tight compartments had been breached by the gash and were filling with water. Thomas Andrews, a naval architect and managing director of design for the Titanic's builders, Harland and Wolff was a passenger on this, the ship's maiden voyage. Together he and Captain Edward Smith toured the damaged areas and determined that at best, the Titanic had about an hour and a half to remain afloat. There were 16 life boats and four "collapsibles" which if filled to capacity could accommodate 1,178 people. The Titanic had nearly her full capacity of 2,435 passengers and approximately 900 crew members. Which meant only one third of those on board could expect to avoid the freezing waters of the North Atlantic. It was, indeed, a dark night.

The first lifeboat to be launched held 28 people; it could have held 65. The law of the sea was then evoked: women and children first! Men would sneak onto the boats anyway. Most of the boats were launched half-full as members of the crew were afraid to overcrowd them. Margaret Brown remained calm and helped people clamber onto the swaying lifeboats. There had been drills for this sort of thing, but few had paid attention to them. It was chaos. Often someone slipped and plunged into the frigid sea; their life expectancy was between 15 and 30 minutes. No adequate evacuation procedures had been in place nor had the crew been trained for such an emergency; the Titanic had been declared unsinkable, so why bother?

The ship had been sinking bow first and gradually this angle increased, making it difficult to maneuver on the deck. Many of the third class passengers where trapped below decks as the ship filled with water and perished without a chance of reaching the lifeboats. At 2:40 AM the rate of sinking increased dramatically and the bow slipped beneath the surface, raising the stern up into the air. Her weight placed so much strain on the keel that the Titanic began to break into two pieces. By now, anyone left on board was doomed. These included Captain Edwards, Thomas Andrews, John Jacob Astor, Jr., and Benjamin Guggenheim. Guggenheim and his valet returned to their staterooms and changed into formal dress, "prepared to go down like gentlemen."

Distress signals and rockets failed to bring help. No one was near enough to reach the sinking ship in time. It was 4:00 AM before the RMS Carpathia reached the scene. They found an ice field with around 20 large icebergs, ice floes and the half-filled lifeboats and debris from the Titanic. There were only 710 survivors.

Margaret Brown had been helping with the lifeboats without regard for her own safety. She had to be forcefully placed in one of the last boats to be launched. Maggie's boat was under the command of Quartermaster Robert Higgins. She grabbed up an oar herself and urged Higgins to return to the sinking ship to pick up people who were in the water. Higgins was afraid the suction from the sinking Titanic would pull down their boat or that people scrambling to get in might swamp them. Brown described Higgins later in an interview as being "with an attitude like someone preaching to the multitude, fanning the air with his hands." He had, she said, "recommenced his tirade of evil forebodings, telling us we were likely to drift for days."

Once on the deck of the Carpathia, Margaret again took charge, organizing food and blankets and compiling a list of the survivors. She raised more than ten thousand dollars in aid from the first class passengers on the Carpathia before it had even reached New York. She became president of the Titanic Survivors' Committee and found, to her chagrin, that she had become famous as the "Heroine of the Titanic." She had been "brined, salted, and pickled in mid ocean," she said. She wrote to her attorney that the "water was fine and swimming good. Neptune was exceedingly kind to me and now I am high and dry." The high-and-dry Mrs. Brown was quoted by a newspaper explaining that her survival was due to the Brown Luck, "We're unsinkable," she said.

Byron Grush

# 5

## The Rum Runner

Stepping on sparkling white sand under the hot Florida sun felt like walking on hot coals. Rose ran across the beach and plunged into the ocean, squealing with glee. Violet had wisely worn sandals and followed more slowly behind, holding Gladys' hand and carrying a toy bucket and shovel. Mother sat in a covered beach chair up on the beach's boardwalk with F. Scott Fitzgerald's novel, *The Beautiful and the Damned*, on her lap; it was the story of a troubled marriage, something Hazel could appreciate. The author's latest novel, *The Great Gatsby*, would be published next month. He and Zelda often stayed at The Breakers when they were in Palm Beach but were presently living in Paris.

The walkway was a solid row of green- and white-striped canvas beach chairs, bulging with beach goers: mostly women wearing fashionable swimwear of sleeveless wool tank suits, similar to those worn by the men but more elaborately detailed with colorful stripes and patterns. Gone were the days when The Breakers' Connie Lewis patrolled the beach checking the ladies' swimming costumes for the slightest appearance of flesh—dark stockings covered legs in those days; now the tank suits stopped at mid-thigh. Practicality had trumped modesty. Even the swimming caps were smaller, appropriate for bobbed hair styles.

On the beach were throngs of sun-worshipers. Games with beach balls were popular. Men and women braved the breaking waves along the pier by venturing out along a long rope. Children played where the ocean lapped up onto the sand depositing the occasional jellyfish or seashell. Gulls swopped arrogantly at picnickers who had dropped the crusts of their sandwiches.

Violet had gotten Gladys situated at the water's edge building sand castles. Did she dare, she wondered, to walk down to the sea wall to see if the body was still there? She could "discover" the gruesome remains, thereby bringing attention to the murder without having to admit she had known it was there all along. But she shouldn't leave Gladys alone so near the breaking waves. People always warned you about the "undertow," didn't they?

In the beach chair next to Hazel sat a Mrs. Jamison Holmes, also from Brooklyn, a fact Hazel discovered from an unavoidable ease dropping—the woman's loud blabbering to a companion seated on her other side was impossible to ignore. Hazel didn't know the woman, and really didn't care to make her acquaintance. Mrs. Holmes was gossiping about some of the other boarders staying at The Breakers. That was mildly interesting, but what caught Hazel's attention was the following:

"Did you hear that they found a body washed up down at Delray Beach. Horrible! It was all decomposed and the face had been nibbled off by fish...they say. They couldn't identify the man, of course, but the police are searching all the hotels for anyone missing. It could have drifted down the coast from just about anywhere...even from here! I can't imagine if anyone was missing that it wouldn't have been reported. You know what I think? It was one of those rum runners. Probably fell off a boat out beyond the twelve-mile limit."

Rum runners! Hazel, like everyone else in the resort area, was aware that the South Florida coast was a hotbed of alcohol smuggling. The most famous rum runner, William McCoy, had been captured two years ago by the U.S. Coast Guard. McCoy had a fast schooner he called the Tomoka with a machine gun mounted on its deck. He picked up rum and Irish or Canadian whiskey and gin from nearby Bimini and anchored just beyond the twelve-mile limit in an area that became known as Rum Row. He never brought the illegal booze to shore; that dangerous business he left to others like Habana

Joe and his fast speed boat. McCoy never watered his whiskey to make it go farther as others did, thus giving rise to the expression, "the real McCoy." But his machine gun was no match for the artillery shell that crossed his bow from the U.S. Coast Guard Cutter Seneca.

Yet as Prohibition remained the law of the land, rum running remained a profitable business. Even sedate West Palm Beach had its speak-easies. The Royal Poinciana Hotel had a bar called Hypocrites' Row. Women weren't allowed, of course, but men could drink, play pool or read a stock market ticker tape there while the ladies had tea in the nearby Palm Room. The bar was entered through a secret hallway off the men's restroom. At The Breakers there was no need for such skulking around. Room service unofficially delivered bottles of the real stuff if you tipped generously.

The cops were making only the smallest of dents in the rum runners' business, but a competitor, a local swamp bandit named John Ashley, known as the King of the Everglades, hijacked so many of their cargoes he nearly put an end to smuggling in South Florida. The Ashley gang robbed banks and had their own stills hidden away in the swamp land. Ashley had raided the rum runners' stronghold at the Bahama's West End; because this was a British Crown colony the act made him an authentic American pirate. His 13 year feud with Palm Beach County sheriffs George and son Robert Baker ended in 1924 when authorities ambushed Ashley and three members of his gang near Roseland. The gangsters were shot attempting to escape while handcuffed, a fact that suggested foul play on the part of the police.

Violet had drafted Rose into watching Gladys while she ran down the beach to the rocks where she expected to find the decaying body of her own gangster, the man who had once worn a pale blue necktie. But all she found were algae-covered boulders and gull droppings. Well, it was just as well. Maybe she had just imagined the entire episode. At least she could now stop being afraid of the piano man, Mr. Jones—if that was really his name. As she pulled off her sandals to walk back along the water's edge, something was going on back at the hotel. Something that would have interested Violet greatly.

Dressed in a dark suit and bowtie and wearing a white panama hat, 37 year-old County Sheriff Robert Baker leaned impatiently against a crutch at the front desk of The Breakers as the desk clerk thumbed through the sign-in ledger. Baker had been appointed

Deputy Sheriff by his father, then Sheriff Charles Baker, in 1909 and had been elected sheriff upon his father's death in 1920. It was Robert who had relentlessly pursued John Ashley and had organized the ambush that ended the swamp bandit's life. Ashley had taunted Robert's father for years, eluding capture and often leaving a bullet at banks that he robbed instructing the bank clerk to "give this to the sheriff." Baker's vendetta against rum runners now continued at a serious pace, in spite of his handicap; while he was Deputy Sheriff, a Black man he had captured shot off his foot, resulting in the amputation of his leg.

Baker, like Mrs. Holmes, believed that the corpse of the man that had washed up on Delray Beach was that of a rum runner. The only clue to his identity was a label from a Chicago clothing store sewn onto his vest and a room key with the logo of The Breakers on it. The clerk finally located a page on which were the signatures of a couple from Chicago, a Mr. and Mrs. Thompson, and another man named Mr. Jones, listing his home residence as the Lexington Hotel in Chicago and his occupation as "salesman." They were the only Midwesterners currently registered at the hotel. A third entry indicated that two men, one named Mr. Smith, had checked out the day before. The home town and the name of the second man were smudged. Baker determined to interview all of them at the earliest opportunity.

Baker was worried about the appearance in Palm Beach of single men from Chicago. Although most of the organized crime connections in South Florida were to mobsters operating from New York and New Jersey, stories of gang warfare in the Windy City concerned him; if the Chicago Outfit came after the rum running business down here there would certainly be a blood bath.

When the Volstead Act took effect in Chicago in January of 1920, the criminal element moved from the protection racket and prostitution to illegal liquor, (continuing the protection racket and prostitution, of course). For a while the rival gangs cooperated with each other and stayed in their respective areas. This brief hiatus from violence was due, in part, to then Mayor Big Bill Thompson's ability to keep the peace. However, everybody wanted a piece of the action: druggists applied for licenses to dispense medicinal liquor; the sales of sacramental wine soared. Speakeasies opened in every neighborhood. Tensions rose.

By February the killings began in earnest. A labor racketeer named Maurice "Mossy" Enright was gunned down near his home. In May, the crime lord Jimmy "Big Jim" Colosimo was killed in the lobby of his restaurant on Wabash Avenue. A possible suspect was Frankie Yale, a New York hit man with ties to Johnny "Papa Johnny" Torrio and his chief lieutenant, Alphonse Capone. Colosimo's gangland funeral was the biggest the city had ever seen. Kneeling at the coffin were Chicago Aldermen Michael "Hinky Dink" Kenna and John J. "Bathhouse" Coughlin.

Torrio took over Colosimo's empire and made a deal with rival crime families to divide the city up into specific territories. The Genna Brothers partnered with Torrio in a bootlegging scheme to bring liquor in from Canada. The only hold-out to the territorial plan was the South Side's "Spike" O'Donnell gang. Within the next few years there would be skirmishes and killings. The O'Donnell gang lost some of its members. In 1924, Al's brother Frank Capone was killed by Cicero Police. Capone then effectively took over the suburban town by placing his thugs at polling places to install corrupt officials into the local government. At one time he pistol-whipped the mayor during a council meeting in order to make a point.

The violence intensified when North Side crime boss Dion O'Banion scammed Johnny Torrio by selling him a brewery he knew was about to be raided by police. Torrio would serve jail time for his ownership of the illegal brewery. O'Banion would be shot point blank in his flower shop on North State Street. The O'Banion gang, now under Earl "Hymie" Weiss, Vince "The Schemer" Drucci and George "Bugs" Moran, started a five-year gang war with Torrio and Capone's Outfit. Some of the gun play was simply bizarre. When hit man Sam "Nails" Morton was killed by being thrown by his horse and kicked, his buddy, Louis "Two Guns" Alterie, shot the horse.

In January of 1925, Weiss, Drucci and Moran followed two limos in which Torrio and Capone were riding. They opened fire killing Torrio's chauffer and his dog but Capone and Torrio were unharmed. Two weeks later they ambushed Torrio again and wounded him. "Bugs" Moran leaned over Torrio to place a bullet in his brain but his gun jammed just as the police arrived. He fled. Torrio recovered from his wounds but it had been the last straw...he turned over his entire empire to Capone and left the business, allegedly taking with him $30,000,000 in cash.

So yes, County Sheriff Robert Baker was very interested in interviewing men from Chicago who were vacationing without their wives or families and who said their names were Jones and Smith. His first interview was with the Thompsons in Room 493. It happened that he shared the elevator to the third floor with Hazel Valentine and her daughters. Violet, fascinated to see a one-legged man, watched Baker hobbling down the corridor. She would have been further fascinated had she been able to ease drop on the conversation that was about to take place.

Big Bill Thompson answered the knock on his door. He had just finished attaching the diamond stick pin he wore in his tie but had not yet donned his coat jacket. He looked the one-legged man up and down, unaware that this was the sheriff. "What ya selling?" he asked. Baker showed him his badge.

"Better come in," Thompson told him. Big Bill was used to dealing with police and politicians and could maneuver through just about any sticky situation when he was on his own turf. He wasn't connected here in Florida, however. And it wouldn't be good to be seen in the hallway being questioned by the sheriff.

"Mr. Thompson," Baker began, still not aware that he was talking to the former mayor of Chicago, "we are investigating the death of a man who may have been staying here at the hotel. We believe he may have been from your home town, so we wonder if you might have been acquainted with the deceased."

"No, the wife and I don't know anybody that is here from

Chicago. Do you have a name?"

"That's just it. We can't identify him. We do think, however, that he may have been involved with rum running. That's serious business down here."

"I've had some familiarity with bootleggers. Don't you know who I am, Sheriff? I'm Bill Thompson. I was mayor of Chicago until the last election when that tee-totaling crusader, Dever, stuffed the ballot boxes. Sit down, Sheriff. Do you want a drink?"

"Sorry, I didn't recognize you. And no, I don't want a drink. I hope you have no alcohol up here."

"Jeez! Well, if I can help you, I will. But I really don't know anything about anything. So."

"What about Mrs. Thompson? Could I talk with her?"

"Maysie has been a bit under the weather. She don't know nothin' anyway. I think this conversation is over."

"We won't stand for any gun play down here, Mayor. This is a peaceful resort town. If your Chicago mobsters come down here looking for trouble it will be the last trouble they'll ever find."

The following morning Violet slipped out of the room to explore once again. She was beginning to understand the layout of the hallways and various wings of the hotel much better than that first day when she had become lost. Today she found the small alcove with the window overlooking the tennis courts and peered out. It was early, but already there were couples batting a small white ball back and forth. As she watched, trying to fathom the rules of the game, she heard someone coming down the adjacent corridor. There were two men engaged in a conversation which Violet simply couldn't ignore. It was the piano man and another man who she would have recognized, had he been wearing a sweat-stained undershirt. They were around the bend in the hallway but coming her way.

"Big Al ain't gonna be happy you canceled Dickson's ticket," said one of the men.

"That goon was a spy, plain and simple. Changing loyalties? …give me a break! It was clean, though. He's feedin' the fishes."

"Yeah? So what's that flatfoot doing poking around? Damn gimpy one-legged yokel!"

"That's right. He's just a local yokel without a clue. A real reuben. But let's say we let it blow over before we contact the Bahama bunch again. You never know how savvy these cowboys are."

"Yeah, I saw him talkin' to the house peeper in the lobby. I wouldn't sell him short. Hey, butt me, will ya?"

The piano man fumbled inside his coat jacket for a package of cigarettes. Opening the jacket exposed his shoulder holster and the brief gleam of blue-black metal.

"Al said no shooting. You ain't packin' heat are you?""

"Don't get the heebie-jeebies. Come on let's get some java and then find some chippies to party with. Okay?"

"Yeah, I guess everything's copacetic. But coffee? Can't we get some hootch around here?"

The two men passed by Violet's position without noticing her. Now she recognized them. Their conversation affirmed her theory that these men were mobsters—guns and everything! And she had been startled by the references to the one-legged flatfoot. So he was a policeman. But did that mean *she* was in trouble? Would she be pinched and sent up the river? Would she have to spill the beans? She searched her memory of every true crime pulp she had ever read under the covers by flashlight. She could be left holding the bag on this one. What to do? Take it on the lam? No, no good. She'd just lay low and mind her own potatoes.

When she had finished her tour of the hallways, instead of taking the elevator down to the lobby, she descended the stairs. On the second floor she skipped around the balcony overlooking the bottom level of the rotunda, a large, pillared, octagonal-shaped room filled with potted palms and bent-wood rocking chairs. She looked up at the vaulted ceiling and imagined herself in a palace from the Arabian Nights. She continued down the last flight of stairs, wide, marble and recently polished to a glow that seemed lit from within although this effect was simply the reflection of sunlight streaming through the surrounding windows of the rotunda. Outside on the long porch were tables set with white linen and fine silver where some of the early-rising guests were having coffee and muffins. Violet suddenly realized she was hungry.

When she returned to the room she could hear her sisters squealing even before she opened the door. There was a man in the room. As the man turned she saw that it was her father. She barely touched the floor as she rushed to jump into his arms.

"Daddy! Oh, Daddy! You came."

Hazel Valentine sat on the bed, her shoulders slumped. She alone was not elated at the arrival of her husband. She had come 1,200 miles to distance herself from him and his indiscretion. She could tell him to leave or even have him thrown out of the room, but somehow, seeing how her daughters had missed him, she began to soften. Just a little. A very little.

"Harry," she said, "you can join the girls and me for breakfast. But after that…"

"Can't we talk?" Harry asked. If silence can be said to have form, the following interlude was as solid as granite. Even Violet felt it; it was as if the very air was impenetrable, thick and stifling. Hazel at last gave a slight nod and then everyone began to move, buttoning clothing, pulling on stockings, tying shoe laces. The lull dissipated for the children. Something inert remained for the parents.

Byron Grush

# 6

## The Saint Patrick's Day Ball

Like most of the public areas of The Breakers, the verandas were lined with large pots containing various species of ornamental palm, bunches of hibiscus or bougainvillea, and other exotic plants. The expansive covered porch where guests went for breakfast was floored with slabs of waxed flagstone; glass-shaded lamps hung from the high ceiling; wicker couches and chairs were set along the exterior wall of the hotel, facing outward toward the many tall palms on the lawn. The Valentines soon found a table near the outside edge of the porch next to a massive wooden pillar. A bright green umbrella provided additional shade and rippled in the morning sea breeze; from their vantage point they had an excellent view of the ocean.

The menu offered fresh fruits of the region: papaya, grapefruit, bananas, strawberries and of course, oranges. Orange juice, grapefruit juice, papaya juice, prune juice, tomato juice—and Violet had to chuckle at this—hot celery broth. Oh, you could order stewed rhubarb or breakfast figs in syrup, oatmeal, pettijohns, muffins, griddle cakes, omelets, fish, steak, calves' liver, lamb chops or just about anything you cared for. Violet ordered the Shredded Wheat.

"I sent her away," Harry told his wife. He wasn't adept at lying but he had summoned what he expected was sufficient sincerity and coupled this with an expression like that of a pet dog being scolded for soiling the carpet.

"Harry...the children. We'll talk later," answered Hazel.

"Talk about what, Mummy?" Violet blurted.

"Nothing. Eat your cereal."

Other guests were appearing on the veranda. Being seated two tables away from the Valentines were Jamison Homes and his wife, Annabel, the woman Hazel had sat next to on the beach the day before. Jamison nodded at Harry as he sat down.

"I know that man," Harry exclaimed. "He comes into the shop now and then looking for rare first editions. I think he's some sort of dentist...the kind that straightens teeth. I should say hello."

As her father stood talking to Jamison Holmes, Violet took the opportunity to quiz her mother about the tension she sensed between her parents. "Are you and Daddy fighting?" she asked.

"No, sweetheart, Mommy's just a bit grumpy this morning."

"Will Daddy be sleeping in our room tonight?"

"I don't know. We'll have to see about that. He may be returning to Brooklyn on the next train."

"Oh, I do so want him to stay!"

"Daddy has to work, Violet. He's very busy right now."

"Are you sure you're not fighting?"

Harry returned to the table. "Holmes just found a copy of Brewster's *Reynard the Fox!* 1701 with blue leather bindings! Damn, I wish I could have sold him that!"

"Harry, don't curse in front of the children."

"I'm sorry, Hazel. I was distracted."

"You seem to get distracted quite easily these days. I tell you what, Harry, why don't you take the children to the beach this morning. I have some shopping to do. You see, I'm going to the Saint Patrick's Day Ball tonight and I haven't a thing to wear. Then, of course, you'll want to catch the afternoon train."

"Shopping!" said Violet. "Oh Mummy, can I come too? I'd love to go to the shops."

There were several shops across the lake in West Palm Beach, most notably, Anthony's on Clematis Street, a three-story building where the entire second floor was devoted to the chicest of chic women's wear. But the Royal Poinciana had a long strip of specialty shops (this was commonly referred to as "Peacock Alley") and was only a brisk walk away along a palm-lined path through gardens and fountains where the strolling patrons of the two luxury hotels paraded day-dressed to the nines. Men in navy sport coats and white trousers; women in pleated skirts and middy blouses with a dropped waist affected by loose hanging belts. And fancier: cream-colored silk and velvet, black satin and lace, paper parasols and hats with feathers—to see and be seen was the order of the day. For Hazel it was an inspiration. Her own best clothing was from Bonwit Teller in New York, but it paled along side the "casual" wear by Callot Soeurs or Lucile in the Palm Beach promenade.

There was an Anthony Brothers next to the pharmacy and an exotic East Indian import shop where one could gaze through glass counter tops at gold jewelry or peruse brass lamps with beaded shades. And many, many women's clothing stores. Hazel wandered down the long hallway, window shopping, appalled by the price tags. Violet followed gaping at rhinestoned flapper evening caps and Tiffany & Company micro-beaded evening bags. She would pull her mother toward one window to point at D'Orsay black satin pumps or low-heeled button-strapped shoes in gold brocade or to another window displaying teddies of crepe-de-chine or rayon, edged with lace.

They entered the shop of Madame Henri. Violet was drawn toward a mannequin wearing a black Chanel evening dress with a square cut neck and transparent draperies over a silk shell, and exclaimed to Mother that "This is the one!" Hazel thought it had too much of a flapper look. There was a silk chiffon Lucile with metallic lace and a Delphos dress by Fortuny with Venetian glass beads that were more to Hazel's liking. In the end she selected what was certainly a Madeleine Vionnet knock-off in green silk and a matching pair of pumps with Louis heels and straps. It was conservative but stylish and dressy, and half the price of the Molyneux or the Paquin that hung next to it on the rack. She added a fringed shawl to drape over her shoulders should the evening become cool.

Later, Hazel and Harry had their talk. The talk didn't advance the cause of marital harmony one iota. "Where are you getting the money for this extravagant holiday and your shopping spree?" Harry had asked although this was certainly not the best approach toward reconciliation.

"You are forgetting I have my own money. From my inheritance."

"We talked of using that to buy a house."

"In Brooklyn? I think not! I'm beginning to like the climate here down south."

"It gets awfully hot here in summer. There are bugs the size of your hand. And alligators. What about my bookstore?"

"Did I invite you?"

And so it went. The issue of the affair was skirted; other things…trivialities…took the forefront of the sparring. Each antagonist looked for chinks in the other's armor, conjuring up dormant remembrances of injustices, slights, self-interests—ancient hurts and angers. Nothing was settled; everything floated in precarious imbalance while neither person could quite push their leaking boat to shore and escape. Nor could they bail themselves out.

"There is a book auction in town this afternoon. Holmes told me about it. I'll be staying over for that and I won't leave until the morning. You'll just have to put up with me. For the sake of the children."

"You can sleep on the divan. I'll tell the children you have a cold."

Preparations for the ball were underway at the Royal Poinciana. Most dances were held in the hotel's ballroom, a large two-level octagonal room just off the rotunda. Leaded glass doors led from the top of a broad staircase to a short hallway of grass-green carpeting lined with potted plants, white wicker furniture, and cuspidors. Just off this hallway was the men's restroom with its hidden entrance to the bar called Hypocrites' Row. On the upper level, just over the main doorway, was a stage for the orchestra. The main floor had accesses to a surrounding porch through a number of arched doorways. Light poured in through windows on the second level giving the space a feeling of monumental classicism: a great domed arena. Japanese lanterns hung from massive beams which stretched from the eight corners of the room toward the center of the high ceiling like spokes of a giant wheel.

Every year there was a major ball held on New Years Eve, George Washington's Birthday and Saint Patrick's Day. There was never an end to musical entertainment, however, as the hotel orchestra played daily on the veranda at The Breakers from 12:15 PM to 1:15 PM, at the Poinciana's Tea Garden from 4:30 PM to 5:30 PM and in its Rotunda from 8:30 PM to 10:30 PM. In the Poinciana's Palm Room, a "Colored Sextet" could be enjoyed from 10:30 PM until midnight—in past winters it had been the Bob Young Sextet featuring vocalist Noble Sissle, a protégé of Eubie Blake's. There were weekly Cake Walks at the Cocoanut Grove where the Darktown Strutters and groups of hotel employees competed for prizes of $25 to $100. Africo-mobile driver Benjamin Pope and his lady friend once won $50 for taking the cake.

This year it was expected that the ballroom would prove too small for the vacationing guests of the two hotels and the seasonal residents of the island and the town. It was relocated to the much larger dining room. Once cleared of chairs and tables, the Royal Poinciana's dining room could accommodate over one thousand dancing couples and still have room for the wallflowers along its colonnaded promenade. Before this could occur, hotel guests worked their way through the canapés and blue point oysters, to a fish course (filet of sea bass or Spanish mackerel sauté), a meat course of terrapin, duck, lamb or prime rib of beef, to the malaga pudding, lady fingers, ice cream, and the final cheese course (Swiss gruyere or Roquefort). After the ball they would be served a late standup snack of consommé, squab roasted over wood coals, lobster or just plain sandwiches (for those who had only a merger appetite).

The hotel orchestra moved into the rotunda to make way for Howard Lanin's Ben Franklin Dance Orchestra, the group that would be playing for the Saint Patrick's Day Ball. Lanin's current recording of "The Craziest Charleston" on Victor records was selling quite well nationally, although the top hit version of this rag-time dance music was by Paul Whiteman and his Orchestra. Lanin was famous for his rendition of "The Black Bottom" and "Melancholy Lou" and could hold his own on any of the year's newly published songs such as "Five Foot Two, Eyes of Blue," "I Found a New Baby," "If You Knew Susie," "Tea For Two," "Yes Sir, That's My Baby," or the Gershwins' "Sweet and Low-Down." Less spirited waltzes and fox trots such as Irving Berlin's "Always" and Ben Black's "Moonlight and Roses," filled out the band's repertoire.

In her room on the second floor of The Breakers, Billie Burke was dressing for the ball, laying out various strings of pearls and other necklaces on the bedspread before making her final choice. Her thoughts went to Ziggy and his shenanigans. Only this last January he had allowed two of his Follies girls to attend the high season right here at Palm Beach—without a thought as to how scandalous it looked or how it reflected on Billie within her Florida social set.

The two starlets, Helen Lee Worthing and Phoebe Lee, were uncommonly beautiful. They had commanded the attention of practically every male on the island, young or old, single or married. But the last laugh was on Ziggy. Helen met a millionaire and never returned to the Follies; Phoebe traveled to Havana collecting diamonds and suiters and gave up dancing. Billie Burke wasn't aware, however, that Phoebe Lee had returned to Palm Springs two days ago and was now sharing a suite of rooms at the Royal Poinciana with the wealthy, aging Oliver Ridge, a rich lumber baron from Wisconsin.

Worthing would go on to Hollywood to star in movies with such notables as John Barrymore. She would be lauded for her extraordinary beauty, until a violent beating by an intruder would leave her with a broken nose and missing teeth. The doctor who would be called to treat her would be a Black man named Dr. Eugene Nelson. Helen would fall madly in love with Nelson and soon marry him, keeping the marriage secret from the public. But the doctor would prove to be a jealous, cruel man who threatened to confine her to an institution for the insane in order to control her. Her life would begin a downward spiral into depression, alcoholic hallucinations, and suicidal tendencies which would later land her in a psychiatric ward. After divorcing the doctor she would sink lower and lower into heroin addiction and virtual poverty, and in 1948 would be found dead from an overdose of barbiturates. Such was the life of this Ziegfeld Girl—a not uncommon story.

As Billie Burke looked over her jewelry, her friend, Marjorie Merriweather Post Hutton, was engaged in a similar activity in her own Palm Beach home. Her jewelry box contained items which were not only valuable…they were legendary. She collected Sèvres porcelain, antique French furniture, golden and jeweled boxes, and items by Fabergé, but the acquisition of famous jewelry was her greatest passion. She would come to own, and one day donate to the National Gem Collection in the Smithsonian, the 30-carat Blue Heart Diamond, the emerald Marie-Louise Diadem and diamond necklace which Napoleon had gifted to his second wife, the 21-carat Maximilian Emerald once belonging to the Austrian archduke

Ferdinand Maximilian Joseph von Hapsburg-Lorraine, the "mad monarch" of Mexico, and the spectacular Cartier necklace of Columbian emeralds set in platinum with diamond links crafted in an Art Deco stylization of Native American jewelry. For the ball tonight she selected a platinum brooch with a 60-carat Mughal emerald surrounded by diamonds.

In room 493 Maysie Thompson was also preparing for the ball. Big Bill was grumbling. He was being dragged to this social affair against his will and had had to cancel a perfectly good poker game. Maysie had purchased a brand new Hot Point Edison electric curling iron just for this trip and she now looked for an outlet to plug the cord into. Big Bill thought it looked like an antique torture device.

"Be careful with that thing," he growled. "You want to burn the hotel down? I don't see why we have to go to this shindig anyway."

"It's something one must do if one wants to belong in society. And anyway, you haven't taken me dancing in a month of Sundays."

"We got plenty of society back in Chicago."

Violet peered from her vantage point behind the tall column. The ball had been underway since 8:30; it was now 9:45. She had had to wait until Rose and Gladys were asleep before she slipped out. Mother had condescended to allow Father to escort her to the ball, most likely for appearances' sake. Violet now watched as her parents negotiated a more than adequate waltz step. She must have been mistaken to think that they were fighting. Was he whispering sweet nothings in her ear at this very moment? No, he was boring her with his description of the book auction he had attended earlier in the afternoon. A rare edition of Charles Dickens' *David Copperfield*, all 20 parts in a leather half-binding complete with advertising sheets, had slipped through his fingers when the bidding had gone astoundingly high. He had, however, acquired a first edition of Rudyard Kipling's *Just So Stories for Little Children*, illustrated by the author and signed. He was as happy as a clam, he told her. She clammed up, still unhappy about his recent infidelity.

Across the room Violet saw Billie Burke engaged in conversation with another woman whom she recognized as Margaret Brown. Brown had approached Billie as she stood talking to a third woman who was elegantly dressed and bejeweled; it was Margaret Merriweather Post Hutton. Hutton had immediately turned and walked away when Brown intruded—an obvious snub. The unsinkable Maggie was still considered a social climber and a hick in certain circles. Billie Burke wasn't as stand-offish as her friend Mrs. Hutton. But the two made an odd tableau, thought Violet, with Brown's stocky form towering over Billie's. Like Beauty and the Beast.

Green crepe paper garlands hung from the vaulted ceiling of the dining-room-turned-ball-room. Violet watched eagerly as Howard Lanin's Ben Franklin Orchestra swung into high tempo for the Charleston contest. Since the day the song had been introduced in the 1923 hit Broadway musical, "Runnin' Wild" it had inspired a dance contest at nearly every event at which it was played. It would, however, soon be surpassed by the Black Bottom as the dance craze of the decade.

Phoebe Lee was on the floor now, sequins shaking and pearls bouncing as she kicked and twisted in a solo version of the dance. The former Follies girl was a cinch to win. Sugar daddy Oliver Ridge sat on the sidelines; his participation would likely bring about a coronary. Phoebe's jay-bird step with arms a-flapping was an inspiration for the twelve year old Violet who watched from behind the column. She studied the moves young women on the dance floor were making and even attempted the rubber legs herself with no sense of self-consciousness.

It was then that the piano man came up behind her and grabbed her by the arm. "Spying are we?" he said, leaning close to her ear.

Violet was instantly wrenched from her flapperesque fantasy and thrown into a terrible trepidation. She could only stammer: "I didn't tell!"

"Oh? You didn't tell what, missy?"

"I mean...I mean...I didn't see anything."

"What was it you didn't see, may I ask?"

"I only meant to say I'm not spying. I'm...I'm watching the dancing. Please let me go. You're hurting me."

The piano man tightened his grip on the girl. "Why don't we go for a little walk and you can tell me all about it?" he said.

"I'll scream if you don't let me go!" Violet doubted, however, that anyone would hear her scream over the blaring of the band. Gathering all the resolve (and strength) she could muster, Violet aimed a well considered kick at the man's groin. The piano man recoiled in pain, releasing his grip on the girl's arm. Violet took off running.

She ran down a long hallway, positive she could hear the footfalls of the piano man behind her. A turn here, a turn there, and soon she found herself in the ballroom, empty and dark now that the dance had been moved into the dining room. The great octagonal chamber was connected to the rest of the hotel but was basically a stand-alone structure. She tried one of the outside doors but it was locked. The only way out was in the direction of her pursuer. She found stairs and climbed to the second floor platform where the hotel orchestra would have been situated during a dance. Here she cowered, afraid even to breathe as the piano man entered the cavernous space below.

Jones, if that was his real name, walked slowly around the periphery, peeking around columns where dim moonlight filtering through windows was the only source of illumination. In an alcove he found a wall switch and suddenly the ballroom was bathed in electric light. "Now I've got you," he muttered.

Violet could watch his progress around the room through the widely spaced balusters of the orchestra loft, but she would be visible to Jones if he looked up. She eased slowly back to crouch behind a folding chair, still sparse camouflage for the frantic fugitive, but better than nothing. Her foot bumped against the chair. The piano man heard the noise and glanced up toward the balcony.

# 7

## The Pier at the Breakers

Hazel shook Rose until she awoke. "Where is your sister?" she demanded. "Where is Violet?"

The Valentines had returned to their room after the dance to discover their eldest child missing. It was about 10:00 PM. Harry attempted to calm Hazel, suggesting that Violet would appear at any moment from whatever childish adventure had prompted her to leave the other children unattended; he wasn't able to convince himself, however, that there was nothing to worry about.

Rose could contribute nothing concrete toward solving the mystery of her missing sister, although she did remember Violet talking about how much she wanted to observe the Saint Patrick's Day Ball—so much so that she might just steal away once Rose and Gladys were asleep.

"Of course!" Harry said. "She's probably down there right now watching them dance the Black Bottom. You stay here and I'll go back and look for her. I have to say, Hazel, sometimes your daughter…"

"Oh, she's my daughter now? She's *your* daughter when she wins an award at school, but she's *my* daughter when she does something like this!"

Harry walked the short distance to the Royal Poinciana

grumbling to himself. As he made a circuit of the dance floor he thought, I should have said, "Yes…you're the bad influence!" There were so many things he should have said. But his anger quickly abated as he began to realize that Violet was nowhere to be seen. The last waltz had been played and waiters were bringing in the cold supper for the few remaining ball-goers. He asked everyone who would talk to him, but no one had seen a young girl.

Benjamin Pope had been waiting by his Africo-mobile outside the Royal Poinciana Hotel. Palm fronds swayed against a sky filled with moonlit clouds; sea birds patrolled the damp beach sand alert for errant crabs. As he leaned dreamily against the wheeled wicker chair Pope noticed the lights come on in the octagon structure that was the ballroom—unusual, for Pope knew the dance had been moved to the dining room. Who was in there, he wondered? A burglar?

The couple he had brought to the ball was still dancing; if they came out now they would just have to wait while Pope investigated. If he ignored the possibility of a break-in and his employers found out, he would surely be fired. Besides, it was boring standing there alone in the dark. The other chair drivers were engaged around the other side of the hotel in a hot game of craps. Pope had declined to join them. Pope no longer gambled. He no longer drank. It wasn't as if he had religion or was a teetotaler—he just didn't have the extra money to indulge in such vices. But catching a burglar in the act would be about as entertaining as things could get around this sedate resort.

The outside doorways were locked this time of night. Pope entered through the front entrance of the hotel proper, crossed through the deserted rotunda and climbed the marble stairs linking the hotel to the balcony of the ballroom where he could get a good view of the big room. Yes, there was a man lurking about down there. Pope called out, "Hey, what you doin' there?" The man ducked behind a pillar. As he turned to descend the stairs to the main floor of the ballroom, Pope saw the girl crouched behind a wooden chair. Violet put her finger to her mouth in a "be quiet" sign. Pope nodded.

Pope was a big man with large shoulders, thick arms, a round head perched on a nearly nonexistent neck and strong hands that looked as if they could crack coconuts as easy as egg shells. He was confident he could best the interloper in a fight should one occur. The man he sought was somewhere here in the gloom, behind this pillar or that one…Pope would find him and drag his sorry posterior down to the security office. But the girl…what was she doing here?

The piano man was an expert at stealth. He quickly shut off the lights returning the ballroom once again to obscure darkness. He easily avoided the lumbering form of the chair driver as the man peered around pillars and surveyed the dim dance floor for unusual shadows. Jones managed to circle around behind Pope without being noticed. His hand crept automatically to the revolver tucked under his suit coat. The loud report of the hand gun would no doubt bring others rushing into the ballroom: he might be caught. So he grasped the revolver by the barrel, hefting it like a cudgel, and brought it down hard against the Black man's skull. Pope crashed to the floor.

Violet witnessed the brutal scene through the balusters on the balcony above. She suppressed a gasp. Her savior was down, a bleeding lump, a black silhouette against the crepuscule murkiness. The only movement was the fleeing shade of the piano man disappearing from view. Violet waited, holding her breath. Once she was sure the man had exited the building she hurried down the stairs, fearful that Benjamin Pope might be dead: the second corpse she would have encountered within only a few days!

Harry Valentine held his daughter, gently rocking her as a torrent of garbled words and a cascade of tears flowed from the frightened girl. Harry's last interrogation of a ball guest had yielded one bit of useful information: someone had seen the lights going on and off in the old ballroom. Might the father benefit by searching for his mischievous child in that deserted place? He had found her bending over Benjamin Pope, trying the stop the blood flowing from a wound on the back of the man's head. Together they had managed to revive the big man and help him to struggle to his feet. Pope had leaned against Harry as he and Violet walked him out of the ballroom and back into the hotel. Now, back in their hotel room at The Breakers, Violet attempted to explain the bizarre circumstances that had led to her being in a deserted building with a bleeding Black man.

"I know who he is…what he did to that other man. Oh, Daddy, I was so scared!"

Little by little Harry pieced the story together: the body on the rocks; the footprints in the sand; the piano man hurrying away from the scene of the crime; the piano man talking to Rose at the Casino; the piano man chasing Violet into the ballroom—the only detail absent from what Violet thought of as her confession was the pale blue necktie.

"We have to tell that policeman what Violet knows," Hazel told her husband.

"I may have to have a little talk with the man first," Harry answered. "There isn't any proof. The man needs to know he can't harass my children and get away with it."

"Harry! The man is a gangster. You're going to get hurt. You can't..."

"We'll go talk to the sheriff first thing tomorrow, Hazel. I promise I won't do anything foolish."

"Mommy...Daddy...can I sleep in your bed with you tonight?" Violet asked. Harry gave Hazel a quizzical glance; she pondered.

"When she needs comforting, she's *our* child," said Harry.

If you live on the west coast you watch the reddening of the horizon as the evening sun sinks against the ocean, turning the tips of waves into licks of flame. You might toast the sunset with your favorite cocktail. On the Florida coast an identical but opposite ritual occurs in the earliest morning hours when pelicans take first flight and the sky turns pink and the sand turns orange. The golden orb peeks marking a new separation between sky and sea; the bluing of one, the greening of the other, the dull grey infinity of the night at last put asunder. You might greet this daily phenomenon with coffee cup in hand.

But few were awake that next morning to partake of the warming and the brightening—the *becoming* of the new day. Few were witness to the avalanche of white-winged gulls rising and riding the updrafts, the lapping of brine, the scrambling of hermit crabs. Harry Valentine had risen early to telephone the sheriff from the lobby and only saw the glow of morning through the dusty windows of the hotel. Big Bill Thompson pulled the covers over his head as Maysie rose early to plug in her curling iron and work on her Marcel wave. They would take breakfast in their room. Patty Burke Ziegfeld shook her mother to wake her, anxious to spend an entire day on the beach, but Billie Burke only groaned and rolled over. Maggie Brown had been up for hours and was gulping coffee with extra cream on the veranda and did see the fresh tint of morning filtering through the spiky leaves of royal palms. But she wasn't impressed; she had seen more spectacular sunrises over the mountains in Colorado, and from the decks of ocean liners. Benjamin Pope stayed home that day, lying prone, chewing aspirin, cursing the loss of a day's pay. And Smith and Jones? Smith and Jones took a long walk down a long, long pier.

The pier at The Breakers stood twelve feet high and extended one thousand feet out into the ocean. In 1911, Henry Flagler had built the Royal Park Bridge, a wooden railroad trestle, across Lake Worth to bring his trains with his customers' private railcars directly to his two hotels on the island. The trains then continued on to the Great Pier, linking passengers to Flagler's P & O Steamship Line which could dock there on the way to Cuba or Nassau. Eventually, as Flagler completed the Florida East Coast Railroad to Key West, the pier became obsolete as a rail terminal. Now it was used for sight-seeing, fishing, and midnight spooning.

Smith and Jones waited at the end of the pier as a sleek, twenty-foot motor boat painted dull grey approached. The speedboat was named the Hurricane. Outfitted with dual 400 horsepower V12 Liberty airplane motors, she could outrun and out maneuver anything the Coast guard had within the twelve-mile limit. Most days her deck would be filled with burlocks: pyramid-shaped stacks of bottles wrapped in burlap and weighted with rock salt. (In the event the boat was stopped, the burlocks would be thrown overboard and recovered later once the salt melted and the bottles floated to the surface.) This morning, however, the Hurricane was empty of contraband and carryied only three men.

One man remained at the wheel of the Bimini boat, its engines idling and ready for a quick take off. The other two climbed the slippery wooden stairs to the top of the pier. Grunts passed for polite greetings between the rum runners and Smith and Jones. Jones stood slightly apart from the other three…indeed, his immaculate double breasted suit and vest contrasted sharply with the oil-stained garb of the boatmen and the usual slovenly attire of Mr. Smith. A knowing light behind his eyes might have betrayed the piano man's special ability at bargaining; but the boatmen weren't here to haggle…they didn't notice.

Two topics were discussed: the quantity of bootleg liquor to be delivered and the location where it would be exchanged for cold hard cash; the price was non-negotiable. The piano man took issue with all of the above. There was an island near Miami which Jones insisted upon. His trucks needed to be filled to capacity, thus requiring additional product. A discount would ensure future purchases—after all, the illegal booze trade to the Windy City was now the sole province of Capone and company. At this last declaration, Mr. Smith shuffled nervously. He turned to whisper something to Jones; the rum runners took notice of the discord between the two men.

"My companion," Jones explained, "disagrees with me that I should appropriate *all* the product you can deliver. He apparently has some allegiance to another party or parties back home that haven't gotten the message. I assure you, I and the people I represent are the only players in this game. What do you say?"

Smith was fuming. He stuttered as he tried to complain. The rum runners conferred, considering the proposal. Finally the lead man replied that a small discount would be acceptable. Jones:

"We have reached an agreement, gentlemen. Very good. There is one more thing…a favor I would ask of you. Since you are going out to sea, would you be so kind as to dispose of a body for me?"

"A body?" one rum runner asked. "What body?"

"This one," said Mr. Jones as his revolver pressed against the temple of Mr. Smith and spat an angry bullet into his brain.

Automobiles had been banned from the island by Henry Flagler many years ago. Even after Flagler's death in 1913, guests were still required to travel by mule-drawn trolley or Africo-mobile. The roads, if they could be called as such, were made of pressed sand or sea shells. But little by little, the roads improved, brick and asphalt appeared, and a few brave souls ventured forth with their infernal smog machines. Many of the residents of the island brought their cars over the bridge for their own convenience regardless of the wishes of the hotels' owners. The Jungle Trail and pedestrian walkways were now in danger of being devoured by the march of transportation progress.

Sheriff Robert C. Baker drove his 1924 Chevrolet Roadster onto Palm Beach Island and right up to the front door of The Breakers. He had traded in his Model-T Ford for the more expensive Chevy with its electric starter and three forward gears; it had considerably more horse-power than the Ford. This came in handy when pursuing rum runners. The only other vehicle present in the hotel driveway was the limousine belonging to E. F. Hutton who was attending to some business in his office while his wife, Margaret, chatted with her friend Billie Burke in the lounge. Baker parked behind the other car and went to the lobby where Harry Valentine was waiting with his daughter.

Violet was at sixes and sevens about what exactly to say to the lawman. She had feelings of shame and guilt and now fear was added to the equation—the sum of it all nearly rendering her numb and unable to speak clearly. Sheriff Baker took his time interviewing the girl, aware that her emotional reaction to her near abduction was close to shock. Harry Valentine added details he had gleaned from his initial talk with Violet and soon Baker, already suspicious of Mr. Jones, felt he had his man.

Except he didn't *have* his man. He had the nearly hysterical testimony of a young girl, which probably wouldn't stand up in court, and no hard evidence. Baker now drove to the house in West Palm Beach where Benjamin Pope was recovering from his attack by the man Baker believed was Mr. Jones. Unfortunately for Baker, Pope hadn't seen the man who had struck him except as a shadowy form in the distant gloom of the ballroom. The sheriff's only hope was to confront Jones and get him to incriminate himself. If the man really was part of the Chicago mob however, it was unlikely he would confess to murder. And there was the small problem of finding him.

Baker returned to the hotel. The desk clerk he had asked to keep an eye out for Smith and Jones looked worried. A fisherman had just come from the pier, he told the Sheriff. The man had said there was fresh blood on the planks, more blood than he had ever seen in one place (and he'd been in the green fields of France in the Great War).

"Fish blood?" asked Baker.

"Would have had to be a whale," answered the desk clerk. "Somebody bled out up there."

"I'll have to hobble out there, I suppose."

"You can't walk there, not with only one good leg. It's a quarter of a mile if it's an inch!"

"Walk? Hell…I'll drive."

"You could drive your car out along the pier. But there ain't enough room to turn it around. You'd have to back up all the way to the beach. Let me get you a chair and a driver."

"Just like being back in the hospital! A lawman in a wheel chair! Maybe I *will* walk."

From a distance the pier looked impossibly fragile, like a long-legged centipede that accidently found itself wading into a large puddle. But the skinny steel posts now pounded by the surf had held up tons of iron and steel as the great steam engines had pulled rail cars along the pier in years not long past. The pier would be damaged so greatly by the Okeechobee Hurricane of 1928 that it would be dismantled but for now it stood tall above forty feet of deep, clear water and was the preferred platform for fishermen after bluefish, amberjacks, sheepheads, Spanish mackerels, and even shark.

Sheriff Baker, reluctantly wheeled to the end of the pier in a wicker chair that made him feel like an invalid, was now examining a large patch of reddish-brown stain still damp and gleaming under the morning sun. Pointless. A waste of time. Nothing to be gained here. These were the thoughts that struck Baker as he gazed out into the wide expanse of ocean, the salt spray from the breakers erupting against the piles to land and swab the boards clean of the crime scene.

Baker had been in law enforcement for 16 years, the last five as sheriff of Palm Beach County. The amputation of his leg had not slowed him down in his relentless pursuit of the criminal element that plagued the area. He was not about to allow gangsters from the Midwest to amplify the problems of the growing resort area. Bootleggers in the swamps, rum runners along the shores, bank robbers, con artists and riff-raff of all sorts feared him. It would be nice, he thought, if he could find some proof linking Jones to the first murder…and to what appeared to be a second one…but sometimes justice was so blind that she needed a little help. This looked like one of those times.

The pier was like a Damascus blade of steel and wood, an exemplar of civilization thrust mercilessly into the soft womb of primordial mother ocean; a fruitless stab at conquering the boundless, immemorial, inevitable dominance of nature. Baker stood on its bloody tip. Overwhelmed by the immensity of sky and sea, the sheriff could only shake his head, spectacularly aware of his own insignificance. He turned to his chair driver: "Wind's picking up something fierce," he said. "There's nothing here. Let's head back."

# 8

## The Curling Iron

Colonel Edward R. Bradley opened his Bradley's Beach Club in 1898. Little by little the small two-story building expanded and now, 27 years later, it stretched out from the shores of Lake Worth, neatly situated between the sprawling Royal Poinciana and the smaller but stately Palm Beach Hotel. One of its dining rooms fronted the lake and was 66 feet long. A long hallway led from an octagonal entry past another, larger dining room, to a spacious ballroom, also octagonal, ringed with pillared arches and set with gaming tables—for Bradley's was a gambling casino.

Gambling was just as illegal as booze in South Florida, but Bradley had styled his establishment as a private club, thereby circumventing the laws of the land. He strictly enforced a set of rules, partly practical and partly elitist, which barred anyone under the age of 26—and anyone living locally—from becoming a member. He forbade drinking and smoking at the gambling tables but allowed both in the dining rooms or on the broad porch at the back of the building. Women were not allowed membership, and had to be in the company of a male member. At first, the fairer sex could not gamble at Bradley's Beach Club, but that changed once Bradley realized that wives and daughters and girl friends were the key to bringing in massive amounts of revenue.

Bradley's Beach Club was decorated in green and white: the colors of the silks worn by the jockeys and horses in Colonel Bradley's racing stables back in Kentucky. The shiny curtains seemed to be made from those same materials. Even the carpets were the same bright shade of green. "Flattering to the women," Bradley would say. Maysie Thompson didn't think so, however. Her color sense, if not offended by the ever prevalent verdant hues, at least yearned for soft pastels of blue or rose. This place was much too masculine for her tastes. But the food was good.

Maysie and Big Bill were seated in the smaller dining room overlooking Lake Mead to enjoy a late lunch. Bill fondled his diamond stick pin between thumb and forefinger as he looked over the menu.

"Gad! These prices!" he exclaimed. It was true. Colonel Bradley served only the best, and therefore the most expensive meals—expensive in order to keep the riff-raff at bay. His chef, Gene Braccho, made frequent trips to New York City, to Delmonico's and Shanley's and returned with purloined menus which were used to duplicate the New York cuisine in the club's kitchen—complete with prices raised at lest ten cents above those of the fanciest New York dining establishments.

"Have a salad, Bill," Maysie told him. "You could lose a little weight, you know." Bill ordered a boneless top loin strip steak with mushrooms and potatoes smothered with grated cheese and buttered bread crumbs. Maysie was eyeing the Lobster Newburg but settled for the chicken á la king.

Big Bill looked up when a man tapped him on the shoulder. The man called Jones stood behind him, dapper and neat but with beads of sweat forming on his brow. "How the hell did you get in here?" Thompson asked.

"Easy. I told them I was your guest."

"Leave, dammit. I can't be seen with you. That sheriff is asking too many questions about you."

"That's the point, Big Bill. I need your help. If the flatfoot wants to know where I was at a certain time…"

Thompson frowned. This man was trouble. Chicago was one thing, Palm Beach was another. Although the luxurious social life was Maysie's passion, Big Bill enjoyed at least the idea of it. He felt relaxed among the wealthy and entitled dwellers in this tropical paradise. It wouldn't do to have his status destroyed by this thug.

"I see. You want an alibi. What's in it for me?"

"A grand if I skip. I have a C-note for you now and the rest can come later if only you will…"

"Not here. Come to my room later this afternoon. Between four and five. Now scram!"

Violet heard music coming from a spot on the beach where a brace of beach-goers was clustered around a bright blue beach umbrella. Then she heard screeching and squawking and other noises that sounded as if someone was violently dismembering one of the island's pelicans. Of course she had to investigate. Drawing closer, she was able to peek between the hairy legs of a man in a dark green bathing suit and to observe the object of the crowd's attention: a man and a woman were seated on a blanket on either side of a large black box topped with a curved speaker horn—a radio! A portable radio!

The man, dressed not in a swim suit but in khaki trousers, stripped sport coat and straw hat, twiddled with the dials on the box and instantly the squawking became a tinny sounding melody. An equally thin and whiney voice announced, "Thank you…thank you! That was the Happiness Boys, folks. And now, before we hear from the Smith Family, a word from Goldy and Dusty, The Gold Dust Twins!"

The signal began to fade. No amount of tweaking of dials seemed able to bring it back. The woman, also dressed in street clothing, a sun hat covering her dark bob, her legs curled beneath her on the beach blanket so that only a pair of low-heeled shoes were visible under her pleated skirt, leaned forward toward the man. "It's all right, Edwin," she said. "The signal isn't very strong here."

"I should be able to get New York, but all I seem to be getting is WJJB out of Saint Petersburg. 'The Land of Perpetual Sunshine!' Ha! That's a laugh."

Edwin and Ester Armstrong were in Palm Springs celebrating their second wedding anniversary. Edwin was a brilliant researcher in the field of radio and had invented the regenerative circuit, the super-regenerative circuit, and the superheterodyne receiver. The large box that now sat between the couple had been Edwin's wedding gift to his new wife: the world's first portable radio. Edwin wasn't satisfied with its performance.

"You know, Ester, the signal is modulated by its amplitude. You get a lot of static and signal overlap. I wonder, it we were to modulate the signal by its frequency instead…"

"Oh Edwin, can't you just relax and enjoy your vacation? Must you always work?," Ester responded.

Edwin Howard Armstrong would indeed go on to develop frequency modulated radio—FM—and change the world of broadcast radio forever. He would become entangled in lawsuits over patent rights with his (more powerful) competitors, and would be ruined financially. In anger and frustration he would strike Ester with a fireplace poker, forcing her to leave him. In January of 1954, in his thirteenth floor New York City apartment, Armstrong would put on his hat and overcoat and a pair of warm gloves, remove the air conditioner from the widow, and leap to his death on the street below. Ester would take over the legal battles and thirteen years later would receive the settlements that Edwin was unable to secure during his lifetime.

A weak signal issued from the speaker horn: a transcribed broadcast from station WLS—all the way from Chicago! Violet squeezed through the crowd to be closer and listen to the broadcast from this new radio station that was owned by Sears, Roebuck and Company. The Maple City Four were singing:

> *Pack up your troubles in your old kit-bag*
> *And smile, smile, smile.*
> *While you've Lucifer to light your fag,*
> *Smile, boys, that's the style.*
> *What's the use of worrying?*
> *It never was worthwhile—so! —*
> *Pack up your troubles in your old kit-bag*
> *And smile, smile, smile.*

The announcer came on just as the signal faded into static: "The WLS Showboat, the Floating Palace of Wonder, back from another merry trip. This is WLS…your Wonderful Listening Spot…broadcasting from Sears and Roebuck, the World's Largest Store."

Sheriff Robert Baker had returned to the house where chair

driver, Benjamin Pope was recuperating from his beating. Did Pope feel well enough to return to The Breakers with him? Did he realize just how important his testimony would be to bring to justice the man named "Jones," the man Baker was certain had committed at least two heinous crimes? Didn't he think he could put aside not actually having seen the man in order to help the sheriff in his pursuit of this despicable criminal? Might he be able to recognize him at a close observation? Sheriff Baker told Pope what the girl, Violet Valentine, had told him. Pope agreed to look at Jones, just in case the sight of the man might jog his memory. Yes…that was what a responsible citizen should do.

Benjamin Pope marveled at how adept the sheriff was at piloting his Chevrolet with only one leg. Shifting gears was a tricky operation but Baker accomplished this with a kind of fluid dance movement, like a one-legged ballerino executing an allegro. Up Clematis Street, past Gruner's department store, Sewell's Hardware and the Sirkin building. Past the Kettler Movie Palace where the feature presentation was the film "Smoldering Fires," staring Pauline Frederick and Laura La Plante—a sizzling soap opera (Violet, of course, knew the plot from her movie magazines). Turning up Royal Poinciana Way and crossing the bridge to the island. Along Flagler Avenue and past the cottages: Ocean View, Surf, Wave Crest, Reef, Nautilus, and Atlantic—some of the private cottages The Breakers Hotel reserved for its most elite guests, the Vanderbilts, the Morgans, the Astors, the Rockefellers, the Carnegies, the Hearsts.

Baker pulled up right in front of the main entrance. "Wait here," he told Pope, "while I find out if Jones is still in the hotel."

Violet, Rose and Gladys sprinted along the patterned rug in the hallway, dripping water and dragging towels still sandy from their day at the beach. Mother had admonished them in no uncertain terms to be back in the room by 4:00 PM; father was packing for his return trip to Brooklyn on the late train and wanted to say goodbye to his daughters. Goodbye? Violet was uneasy, having sensed the renewed tension between her parents this morning. Her own ordeal had brought a brief succession of hostilities, but now…something was afoot. A separation? She ran through the rich storehouse of her mind to check various movie and pulp fiction plots concerning estranged married couples. Did they normally get back together? Or did they end up by strangling each other?

Just as the girls slipped through the door to their room, the elevator dinged to a stop. The piano man, Jones, walked up the hallway, past the girls' room and around the corner to room 493. He knocked. Maysie Thompson opened the door just a crack. "Oh…it's you," she said, closing the door and turning to confront her husband, who was nipping the end from a long, black cigar with a pair of Maysie's cuticle shears.

"That man is here again. I'm leaving to go shopping. I don't want to return to find you embroiled in another poker game!"

"Aw, what's it to ya? Let him in on yer way out, will ya?"

Maysie gone, Big Bill puffing on a Quintero, the red paper band still wrapped around it, Jones stood staring down at the big man—a man he could neither intimidate nor bluff without some kind of advantageous ace up his sleeve. He had offered money, but this might not be enough. The card he would play next would be that of power—a guarantee that the outfit would back Big Bill's next run for mayor. Not only back it…insure it. Jones began to drop names, suggest scenarios, make promises.

"You got the moxie, all right, but you ain't got the clout. Does Alphonse give a shit about your welfare? I doubt it."

"You know I came up through the ranks. I was in the Circus Café Gang, as they called it…you know, Machine-Gun McGurn, Screwy Moore, Tough Tony Capezio and that little punk kid Accardo…them guys. I'm a player. Who do you think held the door when O'Bannion got it from Frankie Yale? Who do you think recruited those street punks for the 42-Gang…that squirt Battaglia and his buddies Caruso and Giancana? Al knows I'm a mover. I get things done. I have his ear."

"You have my money?"

"Big Bill, I got one thing to say…that's the most foul-smelling cigar I ever smelled. What the hell is it?"

Thompson fingered the Quintero, sniffed along its length. "You know what? That smell isn't the cigar. It's a good Cubano and it don't normally smell this bad. Something else…" Both men saw it at the same time: a grey whiff of smoke curling up from the floor by the window. Thompson leaped from his easy chair and brushed the draperies aside. There on the carpet sat Maysie's curling iron. It was red hot and the carpet was smoldering.

"Damn woman's left her curling iron plugged in again!" Thompson ripped the electric cord from the wall socket and stamped out the smoldering carpet. "Coulda burnt the place down. I told her…"

Sheriff Baker hadn't found Jones to be in his room. After knocking repeatedly he used the hotel pass key given him by the desk clerk and entered. There was nothing of interest in the room except a suitcase which sat on the bed, opened, showing signs of having been hastily packed. Baker ruffled through it; again, nothing of interest. Baker looked under the mattress, behind the dresser, at the bottoms of drawers, at the backsides of pictures—nothing of interest. At least he knew that Jones hadn't left the island as yet. It might be time to bring in a few deputies to help to corral the desperado.

Back in the hallway, Baker had a thought: that man, the ex-mayor of Chicago, he claimed he didn't know Jones…but…thugs hung together, didn't they? He didn't remember the location of the man's room or his room number. He would have to return to the lobby. All this activity was making his good leg ache. Sometimes he could feel pain in the missing leg as well—a curious phenomenon which he never mentioned to anyone. No one, he thought, would believe him.

Halfway to the elevator he saw the young girl he had interviewed. She was looking out a window in a little alcove near the end of the hallway. Violet…that was her name. He called to her.

"Mr. Sheriff…hello. I was just watching the tennis players. Do you play tennis?" As soon as she said this, Violet realized her error. She lowered her head, feeling ashamed and embarrassed.

"No, Violet, I do not. I wonder," the sheriff said, "if you may have seen your piano man today. In the hotel."

Violet tried to think. Again she ran through movie and pulp fiction plots she had memorized. Where did the villains hide out? In the barrooms. In the bawdy houses. In an isolated cabin in the mountains. In hotel rooms…

"There is a room they play poker in. I can show you where it is."

Violet remained in the hallway, just around a bend from room 493. She wasn't about to miss anything—this was *real* cops and robbers! When the knock came on the door, Big Bill Thompson roared a "Who is it?" and upon hearing the sheriff's response, motioned for Jones to hide in the clothes closet. Jones slipped his revolver from its holster before disappearing behind the rack of shirts and dresses. He left the closet door open just enough to see out. Violet crept up to stand at the door once Baker had entered. She strained to hear what was being said inside of the room. She caught most, but not all of it.

"I told you I don't know the man. Wanted for murder, is he?"

"I don't believe I ever mentioned that fact. How did you know?"

"Sir, I am the mayor of Chicago...or I was...and I will be again. So watch what you say to me."

"And I am the sheriff of this county. If I find out that you are withholding information in a homicide case, I will charge you with obstruction...and maybe complicity!"

Violet wished she could peek through the keyhole, but the door was equipped with a pin-tumbler Yale lock. There was further conversation, somewhat muffled, but she got the impression that the argument was escalating. There came a loll and then a loud noise like the crack of a stick breaking.

"You idiot! Now look what you've done. I hope you haven't killed him. Although, now that I think about it..."

"Just a little knock on the noggin. He'll come to...and wake up somewhere else if we drag him down the hall, throw him in the elevator...take him..."

"Take him where? Go get that buddy of yours and get him out of here...I don't care where. I just hope he doesn't remember where he was when he got clobbered."

"Maybe I'm getting another idea. Maybe he shouldn't wake up at all."

"I'm leaving. You take care of it...I don't want any part of this. And stay away from me! Go back to Chicago."

Violet heard the door opening. She ran down the corridor and hid behind a potted palm in the little alcove at the hallway's end. Big Bill stormed from his room and headed for the elevator. Inside the room, the piano man, Jones, contemplated his immediate problem. His buddy wasn't around any more to help him. He was on his own. He would certainly feel safer if the sheriff were deceased—but how to dispose of the body without being seen? As he surveyed the room his gaze came to rest on the still warm curling iron that had nearly caused a fire. A fire! On a table next to an ash tray that Big Bill used for his cigars rested a full box of Lucifer matches. Jones took the box and set it on the floor next to the full-length draperies—draperies that surely were flammable. He struck one of the matches and tossed it into the box. A fountain of flame flew upward and ignited the draperies. Laughing to himself, the piano man left the room.

Byron Grush

# 9

## The Breakers Fire

Earlier, when Violet and her sisters had returned to the room to say farewell to their father, Hazel and Harry Valentine were embroiled in an incendiary quarrel. Gladys began to cry. Rose looked at Violet, alarm on her face, a question on her lips—Violet had been the only one of the sisters aware of the strife between their parents. Gladys' sobbing brought the argument to a temporary halt as both adults now understood that their situation, something they might have put off for later and hidden from the children, was out in the open, unavoidably present, indelibly imprinted on the family's future prospects.

Violet put her arm around Gladys. For a few moments, there was only a smoldering silence punctuated by eyelids blinking away tears. Harry went to the bed where his suitcase lay open. He slammed it closed and snapped the catches. This action prompted Violet's impassioned outburst: "Daddy! Please don't go!" Daddy went, first stooping to embrace the girls, then, without looking back, he hurried out the door—and was gone.

Hazel attempted to console the girls but was unable to conceal her anger and frustration with Harry. When she explained that Harry had committed an indiscretion, it appeared that her daughters were beginning to take sides in the matter; they seemed to be siding with their mother. Gladys wasn't sure what an indiscretion was, but it sounded bad. Rose had an inkling, but her curiosity went no further. It was enough to understand that her mother had been hurt. Violet had no end of ideas about exactly what the indiscretion had been. She wasn't convinced of her father's blame in the matter—in novels and in the cinema things were often more complicated—never one-sided. There would be a reconciliation, she was certain. A bit later she slipped out of the room to roam the hallways. It was a good way to concentrate her thoughts, perhaps to concoct a scenario which might bring her parents back together again.

Now she was lurking outside of room 493, eavesdropping on the sheriff as he questioned Big Bill Thompson. When Jones, the piano man, suddenly burst from the room, she nearly let out a cry. Jones hurried past her, either not noticing her or not being concerned by her presence. The door had not closed all the way. Violet peered into he room, saw the flames, saw the prone body of the sheriff—and then she did scream.

Benjamin Pope was anxious. The sheriff was taking a long time in the hotel. Reluctant to remain in the Chevrolet where he was obvious to passersby as a Black man in the back of a police car, Pope decided to leave the vehicle. He walked around the side of the hotel, beneath the tall coconut palms, considering what to do. He could enter the lobby and ask after the sheriff, but he was employed to peddle bicycle chairs up and down the jungle paths…not to mingle with hotel guests or bother the desk clerk. He was supposed to be sick today. Anything he did do would probably result in the termination of his employment.

Pope looked up at the hotel. The siding was painted a pale yellow, contrasting sharply with the building's red shingled roof. It seemed neat and pretty to the Black man, clean and elegant and altogether different from the ramshackle houses in his own neighborhood. Coming to work was a way to escape the squalor and tedium of reality, alien and detached though he might be within this elegant environment. He was, as a low wage worker, a barely necessary element in this realm of the wealthy and powerful (and white) upper classes. Then he saw the smoke issuing from a window on the fourth floor of the south wing.

Marjorie Merriweather Post Hutton and Billie Burke Ziegfeld sat conversing in the lobby of The Breakers. Husband Edward F.

Hutton was waiting, somewhat impatiently, in his car outside, eager to drive to the building site where their elaborate estate Mar-A-Lago was beginning to take shape. While he waited, Hutton took a letter that he had received that morning from his jacket pocket and read it again for the third or fourth time.

The astute businessman always double checked the details of any transaction into which he entered. This communiqué concerned a purchase he was considering as a present for his wife: a four-masted barque named the Hussar. It could carry 32,000 square feet of canvas on 30 sails. In 1931 the Huttons would take possession of her and sail to Europe, entertaining many illustrious guests including Franklin Roosevelt and the Duke and Duchess of Windsor. In 1935, after divorcing Edward, Marjorie would rename this luxury yacht the Sea Cloud and, with her new husband, the American ambassador to Russia, Joseph E. Davis, entertain heads of state and diplomats in its formal dining salon.

Hutton's attention to the letter was interrupted by a banging on the window. It was Marjorie. "Come quickly," she was saying. Hutton stuffed the letter into the glove compartment and opened the door. "There is the smell of smoke in the lobby," Marjorie added. "I think the hotel is on fire!"

Billie Burke's one concern was for Patty. The youngster was alone in their hotel room. Other guests were pouring into the lobby, some in bathing attire, some with faces blackened by soot, all in a state of panic. The pungent odor of smoke was thickening. It stung the eyes, constricted the throat, made breathing difficult. Billie forced her way through the crowd and climbed the stairs to the second floor but when she got to her room she found the door open; Patricia was nowhere to be seen. There was an empty space on the dresser where her jewelry box had been.

Billie searched up and down the hallway for her daughter. People were running this way and that, unsure of the location of the stairs. Some stood in vain at the elevator doors. Many lugged arm-fulls of clothing and other items. Forgetting her own troubles for the moment, Billie began leading people down the stairs.

The Huttons hurried back into the hotel to reach the E. F. Hutton offices where Edward pulled open file drawers and emptied the contents into a cardboard box. A considerable amount of money could be lost if these records were burned. Once they had returned to car, Marjorie looked into Edward's eyes. "We've got to go back," she said. "We've got to help get people out of there." Edward agreed. The blaze seemed confined to the fourth floor of the south wing, but it would surely spread. Every minute counted. The Huttons returned to the hotel to help with the evacuation.

Benjamin Pope had run into the lobby. At this time, no one was as yet aware of the fire. "Where is the sheriff?" he asked the desk clerk. "There is smoke coming from a window on the fourth floor!" The desk clerk was incredulous. This Black man, a chair driver, shouldn't even be in the lobby much less be asking for the sheriff. Just at that moment there came a cry: "Fire in the south wing! Fire in the south wing!" Pandemonium broke out in the lobby. Cries of "Oh my God!" and "My children!" added to the ensuing chaos.

"Quickly," Pope yelled at the desk clerk. "The sheriff…where is he?" The desk clerk pointed. "Fourth floor," he answered.

Hazel Valentine heard the words, "Fire" echoing through the halls. Violet! Where was Violet? When she opened the door she saw that the hallway was full of smoke.

Violet, at first paralyzed by the sight of the fire and the sheriff's unconscious body, overcame a natural impulse to flee and entered the burning room. She leaned over Baker and shook him, hoping he was not dead. Baker was unconscious but breathing…just. Violet grabbed both arms of the man and tried puling him across the floor. He was much too heavy. Now she turned to run to get help. The smoke filling the room was like a veil; for a moment she couldn't see the way out. Suddenly the heat from the burning draperies shattered the window glass. Smoke and flames were sucked out through the opening, hung for seconds in the cool air, then slammed back into the room as if the hotel had become a fire-breathing dragon, inhaling and exhaling. Violet was thrown out into the hall by the burst of super-heated air.

Flames rapidly climbed the wooden siding, blistering paint as they went. The roof began to burn. A brisk wind from off of the ocean pushed the fire across the shingles. From a distance it looked like a prairie fire, led in its progress by billows of black smoke. Across the lake, in West Palm Beach, Harry Valentine stood on the platform of the Florida East Coast Railway station waiting for a train. He glanced in the direction of the island, thinking about the serious mistake he was making by leaving his wife and daughters. Then he saw the smoke.

He had checked his suitcase through to New York. It sat on the loading platform with other baggage. It contained some rare books he had acquired at the auction. Harry decided to leave the suitcase where it was although he knew he would probably miss the train. He had to return to the hotel.

Benjamin Pope reached the fourth floor to find it filled with acrid smoke. He called out for Sheriff Baker. He could barely see as he moved along the hallway. He touched the walls: they felt hot. A small form lay on the carpet before him. Pope plucked Violet from the floor and held her in his arms. "Child," he cried, "is you dead or is you alive?" Violet blinked open her eyes. All she could see was the Black man's huge face, crinkled with concern and beaded with sweat. She had no idea where she was or what was happening to her. "Child!" Pope said once again. Then she remembered.

"The policeman…he's in that room. I tried…you have to save him! Oh please!"

Pope saw that the room was filled with flames. He saw the body on the floor, as yet untouched by the devouring pyre. Carefully he set Violet down. "Are you able to walk?" he asked. She nodded. "Good. Then run. Take the stairs quickly before the fire spreads." Plunging into the inferno, Pope scooped the sheriff's limp body up, throwing him over his shoulders. The big man with his burden and the young girl with her scorched hair and clothing reached the top of the stairs just as a wall of flame burst out of the room. In seconds the hallway was impassable.

Hazel Valentine and her children were on the other side of that wall of flame. They would not be able to reach the stairs. Other people had come from their rooms, dragging their belongings. The sight of the hungry fire licking the walls, the ceiling, the carpet, sparked a panic among the crowd. One woman began to wail. Children were crying. Men looked this way and that for an escape route but in the smoke and the chaos their efforts were useless. That was when Margaret Brown appeared in the corridor.

"Listen! Listen everyone," she called. "You must follow me." The Unsinkable Mrs. Brown then calmly led the entourage to the alcove at the other end of the hall. Swiftly she opened the window and pointed to the fire escape. "Women and children first," she said. To herself she thought: "Another day, another disaster."

It wasn't long before the fire engines arrived. From West Palm Beach, of course, but also from Miami and Fort Pierce. The roof of The Breakers had collapsed and that building was doomed but brave firefighters dragged hoses and poured water into the flames anyway. The wind had whipped across the island carrying red-glowing chunks of the roof and swirling sparks like swarms of fireflies. The roof of the Royal Poinciana ignited. Stores along Flagler Avenue were burning. Bradley's Beach Club was threatened. Several of The Breakers' cottages were consumed by the rampaging conflagration. The firefighters turned their attention to the Royal Poinciana Hotel: this, at least, they would be able to save. But the nearby Palm Beach Hotel had been struck by burning embers, carried by the southeast wind. Its destiny, like that of The Breakers, was to be a furious transformation from elegance into ash.

Starlet Phoebe Lee and her sugar-daddy Oliver Ridge had been at Bradley's when the warning bells started ringing. A small crowd of people were looking out the full-length windows of the gaming room and pointing at the billows of thick black smoke that obscured the usually turquoise sky. As the crowd moved out onto the gabled porch on the southwest side of the building, Phoebe and Oliver Ridge followed. Someone said, "The Breakers is burning!" As a unit, almost like a marching band in formation, the onlookers paraded across the lawns of the Poinciana, across the golf course, and onto the grounds of The Breakers. The Poinciana had not yet caught fire.

Phoebe walked aimlessly among the milieu of millionaires as all stood and watched in disbelief as their pleasure palace erupted in a holocaust of flame: pulsing and exploding tendrils of vaporous hellfire that scorched faces that could not turn away from the sight. All around them was the jetsam of that palace: bundles of clothing, suitcases crammed full of jewelry, artifacts of a privileged lifestyle that had been tossed from windows or dragged down stairways. And now the very air was no longer perfumed by citrus and sea breeze. The very air that Henry James had typified as being made of velvet now was acrid and chokingly insufferable. Fine soot fell like black snow over the reluctant refugees.

The engines came and so did the police cars and the newsreel cameramen. Police arrested several Black men who were watching the blaze, accusing them of looting. It was being rumored that an elderly couple had been trapped on a top floor of the hotel and had perished. The hotel orchestra, having evacuated the building carrying their instruments, set up on the beach and continued to play. A few (the newspaper reporters would call them "flappers") danced. Someone jokingly requested "There Will Be a Hot Time in the Old Town Tonight."

When Big Bill Thompson had left Jones alone in his hotel room with the recumbent Sheriff Baker, he had no idea Jones would devise such an extreme method of body disposal as torching a building. He had assumed Jones would drag the body down the back stairs and dump it somewhere. It would be found, no doubt, and Jones would be suspected of the murder—of that Thompson was sure. He needed to establish his whereabouts in case he was questioned, and for this purpose he made a show of inquiring of the hotel desk clerk as to the whereabouts of Maysie, his wife. He pulled his pocket watch from his vest pocket when the clerk proclaimed that Mrs. Thompson had gone shopping. "Why, it's four-fifteen," Big Bill said loudly. "She should have been back by four." He then informed the desk clerk that he would be seeking her in the shops over at the Poinciana. He did, in fact, gravitate in that direction, but continued on to Bradley's instead of trying to locate the elusive Mrs. Thompson.

Fire engines roared past Harry Valentine's taxi on the bridge between West Palm Beach and the island. Harry's anxiety increased one thousand fold. On the grounds of the burning hotel perhaps as many as five hundred people were milling, searching for family members, collecting belongings, or seeking help for minor burns. Sheriff Baker had been rushed to the hospital along with several people suffering from smoke inhalation. Billie Burke had found Patricia near the beach, clutching the jewelry box. Hazel Valentine and her daughters, Rose and Gladys, had been in the group rescued by Margaret Brown. Their descent down the shaky fire escape would be an adventure Rose would remember and relate proudly to school friends in the years to come. Gladys simply sobbed. Hazel held a vigil near the front door as hotel guests poured from the lobby. At last she spotted Violet and rushed to her.

The girl stood staring into the wall of fire. She imagined it was like floating next to the burning ball of the sun, so close that you couldn't see its exact shape. Sparks and flamelets danced along blacked timbers, dominating her vision. Walls now consisting of thread-thin stringers of charcoal fell, but slowly, as if in a slow-motion film. The fire was a living, breathing thing which undulated and wrapped itself around anything in its path, rendering wood into hot vapor, melting steel and shattering glass. It wasn't satiated easily; it churned through the soot, flinging embers into the wind which drifted across the lawn to land on the innocent palms, converting them to torches.

Back, folks, back. Back onto the beach, out onto the pier. Over there, onto the golf course. Get away. It seemed impossible that there was anything left of the hotel to still burn but the fire persisted into the evening. There would be no delicious meal in the dining room tonight. There would be no comforters or feather-filled pillows or silk sheets for slumbering. Some would be taken into the homes of local residents or accommodated at the undamaged hotels across the lake. Billie Burke and her daughter would find refuge with the Huttons. But many would sleep restlessly tonight, huddled together for warmth, on the golf course.

Harry Valentine searched through the crowd asking this person or that had they seen a woman with three young girls. Most were unable to relate to the question, still stunned, shaking not from the cold but from the heat. Officials herded the onlookers and the hotel evacuees away from the fire. Harry followed. Impossible to find anyone in this mob of misery.

Rugs and draperies had been pulled down as The Breakers burned; this to prevent the spread of the flames. These now became bedding for the sorry souls who were to spend the night sleeping under the stars—if sleep were possible. Were there casualties? On

Sunset Avenue a man climbed onto to the roof of his house to battle the burning ingots that had landed there. He slipped, fell, bashed his brains against the walk, and became the only known victim of the fire. Two hotels now were piles of ash. The Breakers' safe survived but was too hot even to approach. Those who sifted through the rubble looking for scorched jewels were promptly arrested—23 in all, mostly Black men from neighboring towns.

The Palm Beach Hotel was gone. Sidney Maddock, its owner and proprietor, was a ruined man. The hotel would not be rebuilt. The Royal Poinciana was damaged, but not beyond repair. It would reopen, attempting to regain its status as a preferred fashionable destination for the rich and powerful, but it would be overshadowed by a new hotel built to be fireproof: the reincarnated Breakers number three. The Poinciana would close its doors and become a fabled memory.

The new Breakers opened at the end of December in 1926. Designed in the Italian Renaissance style after the Villa Medici in Rome, the seven-story structure featured a 200 foot-long lobby with a high vaulted ceiling painted by Alexander Bonanno, a Florentine Dining room decorated after the Palazzo Davanzati in Florence, sculptural fountains, and portraits of popes, Italian nobles and Native American chiefs.

Big Bill Thompson was approached by authorities investigating the fire when it was learned that the blaze appeared to have originated in his hotel room. He suggested the cause must have been Maysie's curling iron. "Damn fool woman always forgets to unplug that new-fangled contraption."

# 11

## A Trip to the Moon

Violet had always been fascinated by cemeteries. This one had some of the oldest grave stones she had ever seen. She read: "Here lies berried The Body Of Annie Lucassen, Wife Of William Kouwenhove Born the 25 April 1626, died 5 September 1774." And another: "Van Anrie, 1774." And another: "Schenck, 1767." Many of the old stones were blurred through action of weather and time and were unreadable. She looked up at the sharp pointed steeple of the Flatlands Reformed Church. The Greek Revival building housed a massive iron bell that had rung at the death of every American president since George Washington; this was the oldest church in Brooklyn and the third oldest in the State of New York, its original structure having been erected in 1663 and replaced in 1794. Beside the resting places of Dutch settlers were the graves of Native Americans and Free Blacks, some dating to before the founding of Flatlands in the mid-eighteenth century.

Hazel and Harry Valentine were house hunting in the developing neighborhood of Flatlands in the southeast section of Brooklyn. The recent construction of the Junction on Flatbush Avenue had brought rapid transit to the Flatlanders with hourly-running trains, making the semi-rural area more desirable. As yet the section hadn't changed very much, however, as signified by a simple unpaved road called Lott's Lane that still carried horse-driven wagons of farm produce into the small village.

Violet had wandered away from her parents, keeping them in sight, but needing to escape from the still strained exchanges and bickering that was evidenced at each possible housing location. Harry was intrigued by the variety of architecture up and down Hubbard Place but Hazel wanted more of a country feeling...a house set apart a reasonable distance from its neighbors. They argued. The reconciliation Violet had hoped for had come, but remembered strife still lingered and would erupt into petty arguments at the slightest disagreement between the two.

It was a cool morning. The early morning sun set delicate mists rising from the dew-draped graveyard. Violet was not bothered by the ambiance of ancient mourning that seemed to permeate the place. As many of her age, she was attuned to the macabre, welcomed the heavy silence that could be found in a church yard. Long dried tears that once saturated freshly turned earth had brought forth a subtle mildew that repelled, but at the same time beckoned. The girl was entranced, absorbed by the Gothic vapors. Violet had been sheltered from the reality of death by parents, teachers, and clergy; by the fictional romanticism of transfiguration and afterlife. Here was a glimpse into the eternity of silence that awaited. There was something strangely comforting in the inscriptions on the stones: the acknowledgement of a life lived however briefly within the greater truth of endless time. An impossible nostalgia for nothingness gripped her.

It was a lot for the young girl to consider. Her reverie was interrupted by Rose who had sought her out and now delivered a summons from their parents: "Mother needs you to come. We're leaving," Rose told her. "If we're good, Mother said, we could go to Coney Island! Oh...I do so want to go."

Coney Island! The Nickel Empire! The Bowery and the Boardwalk and the Wonder Wheel! And the beach with its throngs of unwashed masses who had worn bathing suits under their clothing for the trip on the subway from Manhattan; they had a nickel for the train but could not afford fifty cents for the bath house. And the food peddlers who strolled illegally among those crowds, dodging the police who would arrest them—if they could be caught. And the off-color sand, pumped onto the beach to extend its area; so what if it didn't match the natural whiteness of the once exclusive ocean front?

Shooting galleries and arcades and freak shows lined the long avenue of the Bowery—you could see Pip and Flip the pinhead sisters from Yucatan (they were Elvira and Jenny Lee Snow and were born in the Bronx and suffered from microcephaly), or Lionel, the Lion-faced Man, or Violetta, the Limbless Woman. You might miss Zip the Pinhead, however. Zip, sometimes billed as the Missing Link or the Monkey Man, was a P. T. Barnum veteran named William Johnson, who wasn't microcephalic at all. He just had a low forehead and was a good actor. He wouldn't be appearing at the Dreamland Circus Sideshow just now. He was down in Dayton Tennessee, at the Scope Monkey Trail where, as a publicity stunt, his abnormal features would be offered up as evidence of the fact of evolution.

Violet feared her parents would steer her and her siblings to the kiddie rides where she would be forced to baby-sit Gladys on the Chanticleer Carousel (it featured chickens and ostriches), or the Dragon's Gorge Scenic Railway ride with its endless tunnels and garishly painted panoramas. She yearned instead for a turn on the Hell Hole, a large spinning barrel that pinned one against its walls as the floor dropped out below, or the Human Roulette Wheel, a flat disk that spun faster and faster until all its riders tumbled off, or the Shoot-the-Chutes, the greatest water slide ever devised—so splendid was the wall of water that arched over the bow of the boat to soak you as you hit the lagoon at the bottom of the slide!

Steeplechase Park was famous for its horse racing coaster track where participants sat on wooden horses attached to parallel rails that dropped from a height of 22 feet over a length of 1700 feet; side by side they could race to the bottom. Luna Park had the Tickler, the Dodge 'Em Cars and the Drop-The-Dips Coaster (soon to be renamed "A Trip To The Moon") that was so high and so fast that lap bars had to be added to prevent people from flying out as it careened around its sharp turns. Along the Boardwalk, the Wonder Wheel was a 150-foot tall Ferris wheel that had cars that would swing back and forth as the wheel revolved, adding to the thrill. Then there was the Thunderbolt.

The Thunderbolt had been constructed just this year. A man named George Moran had bought a narrow strip of land at Bowery Street and West 15th Street on which a beach resort, the Kensington Hotel, had been constructed in 1895. This now became a private residence for his wife, Molly, and their son, Freddy. Moran contracted a famous carnival ride engineer named John Miller and together they designed and built a state-of-the-art steel roller coaster which they called the Thunderbolt. The house remained on the site and the coaster was built right on top of it, its steel beams running right through the house. When the coaster was running, the house would shake, plates would rattle and visitors to the Morans would fear the house might collapse. The Morans would occupy the house until 1988, roller coaster and all.

The line at Nathan's Famous Red Hots stretched around the corner of Surf and Stillwell Streets. While Feltman's (where the hot dog had been invented) charged ten cents for a frankfurter on a bun, Nathan's advertised theirs for a nickel; the once tiny hot dog stand was now expending into a popular and large delicatessen offering sea food and a clam bar as well as the staple tube steaks, chips and soda pop. The Valentines inched their way along the line with the rest of the crowd. The children, anxious to get to the rides, were complaining. It was the sort of tension that triggered Harry and Hazel's animosities toward one another. Small voicings of discourtesy, although muted by the rumble and clatter of the nearby Caterpillar ride, threatened to escalate into harsh and ignoble utterings: barbs flung without regard for eavesdropping bystanders...or for that matter, for the ears of sensitive children. Children whose sense of the trouble between their parents was now acute and worrisome.

Violet had had enough of it. They wouldn't even notice, would they, if she slipped away from the line and took off on her own. Such a wondrous place to explore with all its sights and sounds and people. She backed away from the other children, turned, and hurried down Surf Street toward the entrance to Luna Park. There the entrance gate loomed, two stories high, its twin towers decorated with giant pinwheels and crescent moons—the entrance alone was like something out of the Arabian Nights! The fantasy continued within the park which was filled with towers of exotic shapes. At night (Violet knew, but had never seen,) over 250,000 electric light bulbs covered every surface and shimmered in a cosmos of energy that transported visitors to another world.

The tallest and most ornate tower, studded with 20,000 incandescent electric lights, rose 200 feet high at the end of the lagoon, the very center of the park. From the opposite end of the lagoon, the Shoot-The-Chutes ride deposited its fearless boaters into the tepid water. Everywhere was color: bright verdant greens, translucent crimsons and pomegranates, glowing citrine golds and yellow-oranges, pale periwinkles. Domes and minarets with swirling stripes topped many structures; flags and pennants flew from poles affixed to these. The architecture of each and every building mimicked such a variety of styles…Victorian, Georgian, East Indian, Turkish…that it defied classification. The entrance to the Dragon's Gorge was a huge arch flanked by elaborately carved dragons, with grinning mouths revealing needle-like teeth, their wings spread menacingly to frame the façade. The Red Mill, a tunnel-of-love water ride, was topped by a working Dutch-style windmill.

Violet studied people as they strolled past the circular islands where attractions like the Circle Swings and the Bug were located. They seemed to strut as if they were important delegates to a foreign planet. Here were families with children of all ages, people from all walks of life, in all manner of dress, some big spenders, some on a budget. Now came a man and woman and small child that gave Violet a start. Something about them seemed out of place…wrong. The man and his wife (Violet supposed) were dressed to the nines. Expensive clothes for a day at Coney Island. The man wore a fedora and had a long scar on his cheek. He constantly pulled or pushed the young boy (his son?) along the midway. The wife seemed to be pleading with him, distressed. Then Violet spotted three men, also neatly dressed, following close on the heels of this conspicuous trio. They acted, she thought, like body guards, the way they kept their distance but seemed ready to spring into action at a moment's notice. Was she fantasizing, imagining once again some scenario from a pulp fiction novel? All at once she shuddered as she recognized one of the body guards: it was the piano man!

Alphonse Gabriel Capone, "Scareface" Al Capone, Big Al, boss of the Chicago Outfit, famous gangster and bootlegger, a former member of the kid gang called the Brooklyn Rippers, former member of the James Street Boys, enemy of New York's White Hand gang (after beating one of its members to a bloody pulp), inheritor of Johnny Torrio's Chicago crime empire, briber and corruptor of politicians like Big Bill Thompson, aficionado of the automatic shotgun and the Thompson machine gun, enforcer and orchestrator of Murder Incorporated…was a family man. Al had married Mae Couglin in 1918. They had one child named Albert whom they called "Sonny." Sonny had always been chronically ill, a circumstance which both concerned and embarrassed Big Al. Sonny had lately been suffering from a bad inner ear infection so the Capones had brought the child to New York for a consultation at the hospital. There would eventually be an operation that would fail and leave the child deaf. But now, waiting for an appointment with hospital specialists had made Big Al apprehensive, so Mae had suggested bringing the boy to Coney Island as a way to relax.

Along with "Jones" (we still don't know what his real name was but we suspect it was Italian) there were two other men acting as Al's body guards. They were Alberto Anselmi and Giovanni "John" Scalise, sometimes called the Killer Twins. Anselmi was born in Sicily and had entered the United States illegally only last year. Scalise was also from Sicily and both had inflamed the wrath of anti-mafia officials there, including the up and coming young dictator, Benito Mussolini. Once in America, both ran with the Taylor Street gang in Chicago which was under the control of the Gennas brothers, arch rivals of Capone and Torrio. But defection, like murder, was not above the boys and soon the Gennas were deceased, Dan O'Banion was deceased, and the Killer Twins became associates of Capone and company.

Later in December, after Capone has sent Sonny home to Chicago with Mae, he and the Killer Twins will go to a party at Brooklyn's Adonis Social and Athletic Club at 152 Twentieth Street. This won't be because Al is fond of social events. The speakeasy will host a Christmas party thrown by Frankie Yale, with whom Capone is negotiating new shipments of bootleg booze. Yale has been at odds with a local Irish gangster, Richard "Peg-Leg" Lonergan, leader of the White Hand gang, over control of the waterfront. A rumor will reach Yale that Lonergan plans to crash the party and cause trouble. Capone will tell Yale, "Not to worry. I can fix 'em."

Loneran and five of his thugs will enter the club, drunk and disorderly. There will be ethnic slurs and the men will attempt to intimidate some Irish girls who have arrived with Italian men as their dates. The lights will go out, shots will be fired, and in the aftermath, a very dead Peg-Leg Lonergan will be found with a toothpick still dangling from his mouth and his pistol still holstered and unfired. White Hander Aaron Harms will lie crumpled behind the piano, shot execution style. "Needles" Ferry will end up in the gutter outside the club, a trail of blood marking the floor and sidewalk. James Hart having been shot in the thigh, will manage to crawl out of the club and will be found near Flushing and Throop Avenues by a patrolman. He will claim to have been shot by a passerby. The authorities will arrest, seemingly at random, the bartender and part owner of the club, Jack "Stickem" Stabile, Ralph D'Amato, Frank Pizzo, and Alphonse Capone. Capone, apparently unknown in Brooklyn at this time, will be referred to in a newspaper article as the club's bouncer. All those arrested will skate due to a lack of witnesses even though the club was jam-packed with patrons at the time. Just another day at Murder, Inc.

"When I was a boy," Al was telling Sonny as they walked along, "we used to come down here to Steeplechase Park to the Blow Hole. You could watch as people filed through and when a dame got over the Blow Hole, a gust of wind blew her skirts up. We loved that. Then this clown guy would prod them in the butt…I think he used a cattle prod."

"Oh, Al…the boy doesn't need to hear such things. He's only six, for Pete's sake!" said Mae.

"He's old enough to learn what it is to be a man. You coddle him too much. That's why he's so sickly. We should go over to the shooting gallery or maybe that place you throw baseballs to make a pig slide down a chute."

Mae knew when it was useless to argue with the man. She said nothing in response, but her thoughts mingled anger with trepidation. Al needed his son to grow to manhood…as Al defined it…in order to inherit his father's empire. That was normal…wasn't it? She would never win an argument with him and reprisals for disagreeing too strongly could be painful. Not that Al didn't love his beautiful wife, but a man's home was his castle…wasn't it?

Violet hoped that the piano man wouldn't recognize her. Perhaps she could fade into the crowd, maybe walk closely next to some family as if she belonged to them. But there was no one close by and the Capone entourage was between her and the park entrance. In fact, they were walking toward her! It was just a matter of time before

Jones would see her. Would he try to harm her here in such a public place? Violet didn't wait to find out. The Circle Swings were within a few feet and the ride was about to start. She hurried to jump onto one of the remaining empty seats, much to the consternation of the ride operator. Soon she was whirling swiftly around as the centrifugal force of the ride forced the swings up and out like the opening of a giant umbrella. The park, its buildings, flags and lights became a blur. She might, under other circumstances, have enjoyed this immensely, but now all she could do was tightly grip the chains that held her seat until her knuckles turned white.

Gladys Valentine tugged on her mother's skirts. "Mummy," she said, "where's Violet?" Hazel looked around in horror: the child was missing. Thoughts of the girl lost in this rough environment, of possible abduction or accident...

"Harry!" she managed to half-yell, half-cry. Then Rose offered this: "She walked away...down the street. I think she went to the park." Harry and Hazel looked at each other, this time without recrimination or censure. A truce by overwhelming guilt is still a truce. Concern now led to action. Harry started off toward the park entrance. "We're all coming with you," said Hazel.

The girl was stationary, the world spun around her. It all rushed past, the buildings and the people, at an impossible angle. Then the swings began to slow. They dropped as the speed of the ride decreased and soon Violet was able to make out individual faces in the crowd lining the exhibit's fence. The world was upright again and no longer blurred. Her swing came to a halt and she scanned the waiting crowd. He was there! Leaning on the fence, next to the exit, watching her, was her piano man.

She ran to the side opposite the exit and climbed the fence. Her dress caught on one of the pickets and tore. She ran past the ride called the Witching Waves with its undulating floor that propelled cars around an oval track. She ran to the Drop-The-Dips roller coaster and could run no more: that was the extent of the park property—it was a dead end. She turned...yes, he was following her. Quickly she climbed into the forward most car. The attendant closed the lap bar, securing her to the seat. The coaster began to creep forward. Violet was frantic. The piano man would be waiting at the exit for her. Stupid! But as she turned to look back she saw a sight that made a shiver run up her spine. The piano man was sitting in a car several cars behind her. The coaster began its initial climb, clickity-clack to the height of sixty feet.

Byron Grush

# 11

## The House on Hubbard Place

Drop-The-Dips would be renamed "A Trip to the Moon" after the park's first, most famous, and most profitable scenic ride (now defunct—its entertainment value eclipsed by the advent of motion picture shows). Already the coaster's crisp yellow and blue painted cars had been covered over with a deep satin blue and embellished with stars and comets rendered in sparkling silver aluminum paint. It stood majestically a lattice-work of white-washed wooden struts which creaked and groaned at the passage of the coaster train. Each morning a grizzled but muscular man named Morton O'Malley (he'd been with the park since its inception) climbed up the structure using the ties as a ladder. It was O'Malley's duty to inspect the rails for defects. There hadn't been any accidental deaths on the Drop-The-Dips—at least not yet.

Violet sat in the very front car; Jones, the piano man, had jumped onto the coaster just as it began to move and was four cars back. Each individual two-seater car, which could hold four to six people, was connected to the next by a flexible coupling so that the train could negotiate the sharp turns and steep drops without buckling. This added a small amount of space between cars. Violet knew Jones was too far away to reach out and grab her, but his presence rattled her all the same. When the ride would come to an end...

The coaster angled upward, climbing toward the top of the first great pinnacle, sixty feet above the floor of the park. A unique mechanism of whirling gears whose teeth meshed with the underside of the cars propelled the train with a jerking, clattering motion. This only made Violet more nervous. As her car reached the top she turned to look at Jones. What she saw increased her fear two-fold: Jones had taken advantage of the train's slow movement and sharp angle to climb out of his car and cross over the space to the next. He was brushing past that car's occupants and was about to climb into the next car when the coaster suddenly plunged down the first hill. Jones was flung backwards onto the seat. Riders screamed with joy at the exhilaration of the swift drop—a real heart-attack ride, they called it. Violet screamed as well, but not from excitement.

"What the hell?" exclaimed a man in the car Jones had entered. The man's straw hat had been knocked off as Jones fell backwards, and it now swirled and sailed down, down, like an oak leaf floating in an autumn wind. Jones picked himself up and waited for the coaster to begin to climb the next hill. At the top the tracks curved in a long horseshoe turn with a subtle incline. Perfect for climbing from car to car. Jones managed to reduce his distance from the girl by another car before the coaster swung into the next drop.

Violet had been on roller coasters before, but never one this fast. It was like riding on the back of a bucking bronco. She didn't know if she was more frightened of the piano man or of the coaster. Think pleasant thoughts—take your mind off of your fears—she told herself. She imagined herself and her family sitting down to dinner at that nice house on Hubbard Place her father wanted to buy. Her grandmother's china and her green crystal goblets arrayed the round oak table—they'd had to put in the leaf because of the guests. She hadn't known her parents knew so many movie stars! To her left were Clara Bow and John Gilbert; what a grand couple they made! Across the table sat her favorite cowboy actor, Tom Mix. Oh, Mister Mix, she imagined she would say, could you help me? There's this gangster that's trying to kill me...

Jones had climbed across into the next car, elbowing the man and woman sitting there. "Now see here!" yelled the man, barely audible over the coaster's clatter. Jones swung at him, clenched fist connecting with his jaw. A trickle of blood ran from the man's lip. The woman grabbed her companion's arm. She was crying. Was she wife or girlfriend? Jones looked at the both of them with scorn. "Take care of yer doopy boyfriend, Babe," Jones said. It was too much for the man. He threw a haymaker at the piano man's face. That was a mistake. Out came Jones' revolver.

Hazel and Harry had entered Luna Park with Rose and Gladys in tow. Where to begin to find Violet? "Do you think she'd be on one of the rides?" Hazel asked. "Did she have any money?"

"I gave her some money to spend on cotton candy," answered Harry. "Several quarters. Which rides do you think she'd go on?"

The Valentines were certainly in a quandary. It was huge park. The very sureality of the surroundings was daunting. Lights flashed, music blared from every corner, the machinery of the rides ground out incongruous harmonies of screeching wheels and wheezing engines. Balloon venders and candy venders wound their way through throngs of vacationers, further confounding the possibility of locating the errant girl.

"The Shoot-The-Chutes," said Rose. "That's where I'd go. She'd hate the Merry-Go-Round or the Tunnel of Love. The Chutes would be thrilling. Can *we* go?"

"We are looking for your sister," Hazel scolded. Obviously Rose wasn't taking this seriously enough. "Look, there's a walkway across the lagoon. We can watch the boats from there."

"Good," said Harry. "You and the children go out on the walkway. I'm going to look around at the other rides."

Jostling his way through the crowds, Harry was struck by the impossibility of finding his daughter in this bewildering milieu. He stood for a while in front of the Dragon's Gorge. The monstrous countenances of the two guardian beasts at the threshold unnerved him. Luna Park's wonderland environment was working its persuasive fantasies on him...and not in an entertaining way. He watched as the Wonder Wheel revolved, cars slipping back and forth. He could make out faces...none of them belonged to Violet. Music was issuing from speakers at the entrance to the Red Mill. An old popular song was playing:

> *We'll take a trip up to the moon*
> *For that is the place for a lark*
> *So meet me down at Luna, Lena*
> *Down at Luna Park*

Harry crossed to the far side of the park. There he noticed a crowd of people milling about by the side of a roller coaster, many of them gesturing, pointing up at the racing coaster. When he looked up, he could just make out two figures standing, and apparently fighting, in one of the forward cars.

"Roger," the woman had said as Jones climbed onto the next car, "that man is going for that girl in the forward car! You've got to help her!" The look she gave to her companion was compelling, but...

"He's got a gun, Doris! I did what I could, but I'm not going to get shot." Black and oily, gleaming brass-tipped bullets clearly visible within the barrel, the revolver Jones had held on Roger had been sufficiently intimidating to cower the would-be hero.

Jones pocketed the gun and continued his pursuit of the girl. There was now only one car left between him and Violet.

"Maybe...maybe if I take him by surprise while his back is to us," Roger said. "Oh, hell. Here I go!"

The coaster was descending a steep drop. Jones was waiting for the momentary lull that would come at the bottom before the train started back up the next hill. Roger didn't wait. He leaped the last few feet into the car and wrapped his arms around Jones in a bear hug, pinning the man's arms before he could reach for the gun. But Jones twisted rapidly from side, breaking Roger's grip. He again went for his gun.

At the bottom of the drop both men were thrown off balance. Jones realized that even at close quarters, his shot would probably go wild. He swung the heavy revolver, connecting with Roger's forehead. Roger went down.

Violet had been watching the struggle. As Roger fell unconscious back onto the seat, she let out a cry. She couldn't hear it, but the crowd watching below echoed her hysterics. Jones now crossed over to the car directly behind Violet's. It was empty. There was no one near enough to help her now. Roger lay crumpled in the car Jones had just left; Doris tried to summon the courage to climb across the space between cars to reach her man, but froze as she saw the tracks rushing beneath them.

Below on the park grounds Harry had finally seen that it was Violet sitting in the forward car. He now saw Jones edging toward her. The crowd saw it too and shouted and wailed and wrung their hands in frustration. Harry felt helpless. He ran to the Drop-The-Dips attendant and demanded that he stop the roller coaster. "I can't stop it," the attendant said. "It's not got a motor. All gravity and the like."

"Then call the police," said Harry. What the police would be able to do, Harry didn't know, but something had to be done. Maybe they'd have a sharp-shooter that could pick off the man before he could harm Violet. Maybe...if they got there soon enough.

Jones considered his gun. The girl was trapped; he could easily place a bullet between her eyes. But that would be too quick. He wanted to see the fear on her face, wanted to hear her plead for mercy. The coaster was finishing its climb up the last hill on the course. Ahead lay a horseshoe turn and one final plunge. Jones entered the car where Violet was crouched as close to the side of the car as she could get, as if that afforded some sort of shelter. As he came closer she beat her fists against the large man. Jones plucked her from under the lap bar. He held her in his strong hands and moved toward the edge of the car. "You're going to learn to fly," he said.

Morton O'Malley hadn't missed a day of work in all his years at Luna Park. Not until this morning. He had lain in bed moaning and clutching his abdomen. It wasn't just a stomach ache this time. It was his appendix. His wife, Margo, had run to fetch Doctor Travis. There would be a trip in an ambulance and an operation to remove the ruptured organ. O'Malley wouldn't make that climb up the tracks of the Drop-The-Dips today. He wouldn't see the small fracture in the rail on the south horseshoe turn that would worsen as the coaster traveled over it so many times that morning. He wouldn't be able to warn the park manager to shut down the roller coaster. He wouldn't be able to prevent what was about to happen.

As the forward car hit the fracture it derailed. It was just at the middle of the turn and the momentum of the other cars pushed it perilously close to the edge. The front car tipped and leaned against the frail wooden railing which began to crack. Forward movement of the train had ceased but it now rocked dangerously toward the precipice. The painted silver stars flashed in the sunlight. People in the other cars were panicking, attempting to climb out of the cars before the entire coaster careened over the edge and fell sixty feet to the pavement below. The watching crowd screamed. Violet screamed.

Jones had lost his balance. He had had to release the girl before her additional weight threw them both from the car. Now as he came for her again the railing broke and the front car tilted and began to slip over the edge. Violet pushed at Jones with all her strength. It was an involuntary action, born of panic and probably would have had little effect without the tipping of the car. But it was just enough. The big man toppled, fell, bounced against the scaffolding of the roller coaster...once, twice...there were horrible sounds like birds flying against window panes. Then in what seemed like a slow-motion dive, arms spread like wings, a mask of terror on his face, he fell, landed, and became a mass of broken, bleeding flesh on the pavement in front of the horrified onlookers.

\* \* \*

Violet was to get her dinner party in the new house on Hubbard Place, although not peopled by movie stars. The house was one of a row of two-story buildings built around the turn of the century, affording the grace and craftsmanship of Dutch Colonial Revivalism. At first Hazel hated the place, its dormers and its eaves like scowling faces, its close proximity to neighboring buildings. But the charming sun room at the rear of the house had won her over. Here at last was a place she could escape the tedium of the city, with a view of the garden she planned to add in the little yard.

Violet and her sisters loved the polished oak staircase with its banisters and the small square landing half-way down where the stairway turned at a right angle. The landing would be home to dolls and their tea parties. A transom over the front door passed beams of sunlight into the parlor, except during dull grey winter days. All in all, the house was bright and cheery. Harry's commute to the bookstore was of minimal time and expense. The little family was settled in at last—with no more prospects of horrendous adventure in the offing.

Violet's nearly catatonic behavior after the incident at Luna Park had been of such a concern that doctors had been called to examine her. One, a specialist from New York Hospital, had even recommended shock treatments. Hazel balked at this. The purchase of a tiger-striped kitten was tried. A trip to the Finger Lakes was offered to the girl who in the past would have jumped at the chance. Nothing could stir her from the doldrums of depression and fatigue that plagued her.

Her parents began to leave her to her own devices…which included staring blankly out the window. Hazel renewed her campaign for moving from Brooklyn Heights and dragged Harry back to Flatbush and the Flatlands to hunt for houses. By the fall, the couple had placed a down payment on the house on Hubbard Place and they were shopping for furniture. Perhaps it was this move that jogged Violet back into the real world from which she had withdrawn. Violet would tell you, however, it was Gladys, the youngest of the siblings, the one person in the family who never gave up on Violet, who should be given credit for her revival.

Violet would sit, her mind reviewing the rescue from the roller coaster when she was carried down the steep fire truck ladder by (she added this from her own wishful thinking) the strong, handsome fire fighter. This was the only memory she allowed herself and the blocking of all else from that period was the cause of her paralyzing melancholy. Gladys had urged her to help explore the new house— she was certain it was the realm of sprites and fairies who hid behind secret panels or possibly behind the drapes. Violet finally laughed. Little by little she regained her composure. Now she was again the old Violet, spirited, enthusiastic, even effervescent when she could interact with the rest of the family. Or with visitors.

The dinner party guests were Harry's literary friends, Howard Lovecraft and Frank Belknap Long. A strange aggregation for a house warming, but in addition it was a celebration honoring the finished manuscript of Lovecraft's latest novel, "The Horror at Red Hook." This story of a police detective who discovers demonic rituals going on in a Red Hook apartment which in turn point to the horrific existence of an evil entity dwelling below the city— something ancient and other-worldly—had contributed (once Harry read the manuscript to her) to Hazel's anxiety about Brooklyn Heights and to her argument for moving.

"Howard is looking for a publisher at present," Frank Belknap Long was saying. "I keep urging Howard to talk to my editor, Farnsworth Wright. He has a publication called 'Weird Tales' that I think would be an appropriate venue for Howard's work."

"Do you write horror stories also, Mr. Long?" asked Hazel.

"Frank...please. No, I write what we call Science Fantasy. I'm sort of H. G. Wells to Howard's Edgar Alan Poe."

"Say rather, my Nathaniel Hawthorne to your Ambrose Bierce," added Lovecraft.

"Or my Jules Verne to your..."

"H. P. Lovecraft," interjected Harry. "I thought," he continued, "your device of the smuggling tunnels under the city connecting the waterfront to the occult church was brilliant."

"I always knew there was something ugly about Red Hook...and so close to the Heights!" exclaimed Hazel.

"Yes, a decrepit place peopled with unsavory people. An obvious setting for evil incarnated," answered Lovecraft.

"Mr. Lovecraft," Violet piped up, "why do you write *horror* stories?"

"Well, little lady," Lovecraft answered (Violet was thrilled at being addressed as "little lady"), "I don't think *real* life is exciting enough."

A lot you know, thought Violet.

The weather was turning. Already red and brown leaves swirled in up-and-down gusts of cool crisp wind, a harbinger of winter's inevitable approach. Violet donned her jacket and practically flew out the side door and down the short alley between the houses, her avenue to the back yard. There was a swing set there that drew her.

She crunched through the dried leaves that had blown into little heaps along the alley way. As she turned into the yard, however, she stopped short. There was a hole in the yard. Apparently it was a sink hole, opened by movement of unstable earth beneath the property. It hadn't been there before.

She approached the edge and stared down into the hole…was that a tunnel leading off from the bottom of the hole? It almost seemed as though the tunnel was lined with bricks. What had that author said about Brooklyn? Tunnels connecting the waterfront with the inner city? Smuggler's tunnels where grossly demonic entities lurked? Well, this wasn't Red Hook. But it was near the ocean, near enough that maybe…

Violet stood for a moment considering this. She could return to the house and procure a flashlight. The hole wasn't so deep that she couldn't climb down. And that tunnel just cried out to her to be explored. Father was at the store, Mother had taken Gladys and Rose with her on a shopping trip. Violet wouldn't be missed, would she, if she just…

Byron Grush

# Afterword

The inspiration for this little story came from two found images: an old postcard showing the famous hotel in Palm Beach, Florida, called The Breakers, and an old photograph of three young girls seated on a rock, taken around the time that this story takes place. You can see these on the cover—I combined the girl's photo with another postcard image of the pier at The Breakers. The history of the hotel is rich, being the haunt of wealthy American businessmen, movie stars, and gangsters. It burned twice and was rebuilt each time as a more elaborate and decadent edifice than before.

The events related to the hotel fire are based on newspaper articles and other documents of eyewitness accounts. Most authorities believe that the fire started in Mrs. Thompson's room. She had left a curling iron plugged in and unattended, or so the story goes. Apparently these "new fangled gadgets" were prone to over-heating. Another theory places the blame on faulty wiring within the hotel's walls. Clearly, the practice of building all-wooden edifices hastened the fiery destruction of The Breakers and other buildings near it. The fire departments that hurried to the fires that afternoon are credited with heroic work—but the blaze was beyond their control.

Many of the characters in the story were real people. William Hale Thompson (May 14, 1869 – March 19, 1944) was Mayor of Chicago from 1915 to 1923 and from 1927 to 1931. His ties to organized crime are legendary and he is considered one of the most unethical politicians in the history of these United States. Alfonse

"Scarface" Capone, "Big Jim" Colosimo, "Papa Johnny" Torrio, Frankie Yale, Dion O'Banion, the Gennas, "Bugs" Moran, Earl "Hymie" Weiss, John Scalise and Albert Anselmi (the Killer Twins), and the famous "Lords of the Levee," Michael "Hinky Dink" Kenna and John J. "Bathhouse" Coughlin, were *all too real*. Travel abroad and introduce yourself as being from Chicago—you will be greeted with: "Ah…Chicago! Yes…Al Capone…bang, bang!"

Of Billie Burke and Florenz Ziegfeld much has been written. The woman most famous as the "Glinda the Good Witch" had a notable career in movies and on the stage long before movies could "talk." She wore gowns by Lucille and was quite a trend setter during the teens and the twenties. Ziggy…well, there are at least three movies about his life and escapades. Billie must have had a lot to put up with. Their daughter, Patricia, wrote an autobiography in 1963 entitled, *The Ziegfelds' Girl: Confessions of an Abnormally Happy Childhood* which chronicled some of the off-stage antics of her father and mother. For another glimpse into the world of Billie Burke, see *Mrs. Ziegfeld: The Public and Private Lives of Billie Burke* by Grant Hayter-Menzies.

Another remarkable and beautiful woman that frequented Palm Beach was Mrs. Marjorie Merriweather Post Close Hutton Davies May (that's four marriges). At the time of our story she was the wealthiest woman in the United States. She became one of the most influential of American women ranking just slightly behind Eleanor Roosevelt. She was born in Springfield, Illinois in 1887. Her father, C. W. Post was an invalid when together they moved to Battlecreek, Michigan. Her earliest memories were of gluing together cereal boxes in the family barn. C. W. Post created a multi-million dollar business empire and taught his daughter the business. She later expanded Post Cereals into what is now General Foods. For more on Marojorie see *American Empress: The Life and Times of Marjorie Merriweather Post* by Nancy Rubin Stuart.

Margaret Tobin, the "Unsinkable Molly Brown," was born in a three-bedroom cottage in Hannibal, Missouri. Her rise to wealth and prominence was of a story-book nature—she called it "the luck of the Browns." Her devotion to causes and her courage under what must have been enormous stress during the sinking of the Titanic and the fire at The Breakers places her among the legendary heroines of the twentieth century. Brown ran for the senate twice, before women even had the vote. During World War I she worked in

France with the American Committee for Devastated France helping wounded soldiers. She was awarded the French Légion d'Honneur. She was a feminist and a philanthropist, a humanitarian and one tough broad. See *Molly Brown: Unraveling the Myth* by Kristen Iversen and *Heroine of the Titanic: the Real Unsinkable Molly Brown* by Elaine Landau.

Rum-runner William S. McCoy, "Swamp Bandit" John H. Ashley and his Ashley gang, and many others of their ilk ran illegal booze from Ashley's stills in the Everglades and from Bimini in the Bahamas. Ashley took every opportunity he could to raid his competitors' holdings. Sheriff George B. Baker and his son, (later) Sheriff Robert C. Baker, carried on what was essentially a war on the bootleggers. Robert indeed brought Ashley to justice…of a kind. He did lose a leg but continued his service to the county for many years. Whether or not he was present at the fire at The Breakers is conjecture. He makes a good hero and foil for the baddies in the story, however.

Speaking of "baddies," Mr. Jones and Mr. Smith and their unnamed and very water-logged corpse of a companion are figments of my imagination. Violet and her family are also fictional and not based on anyone you or I might know. The Africo-mobile driver, Benjamin Pope is fictional but much like I imagined a Black man working in the Deep South in the mid-twenties might be. The story of the burning of the workers' town called the Styx may be party myth, but the local lynching happened as I described it. Mr. and Mrs. Jamison Holmes, the book collector and his wife, are made up people, but Helen Lee Worthing and Phoebe Lee, the Ziegfeld girls were real. There was, however, no lumber baron from Wisconsin named Oliver Ridge. Edwin and Ester Armstrong, radio inventor and his wife, did vacation on their honeymoon at Palm Beach. His tragic end was as I described it in the narrative.

The Kalem Club was a New York literary circle whose member's names all began with K, L, or M. It revolved around Howard Philip Lovecaft who spent the years from 1924 to 1926 living in Brooklyn. Frank Belknap Long, another writer of fantasy fiction, was a close friend and frequent visitor to Lovecraft's haunt. I placed meetings of the Kalem Club in Harry Valentine's bookstore, but if the group ever met formally it was elsewhere. Lovecraft published "The Horror at Red Hook" in 1927.

And Violet? Will she have further adventures in some underground realm where evil incarnate may lurk? We shall have to wait and see. The Coney Island of her era may, with its elaborate décor, have presented to the girl fantasies beyond our imaginings—a façade of exoticism and unexpressed desires, thrills literal and subliminal—but what other arcane delicacies of the extraordinary await our young protagonist? There is something universal about this entity we have scripted as "Violet," a female on the verge of maturity yet lingering reluctantly in a fantasy world not uncommon, not unforeseen, not fully understood; an entity equally appropriate for interaction with fairyland or the netherworld, with heaven or with hell.

# About the Author

Byron Grush was born and raised in Naperville, Illinois, just southwest of Chicago. He is a third generation native of that town. Grush studied art and design at the University of Illinois and filmmaking at the School of the Art Institute of Chicago. At the Art Institute he was a student of Gregory Markopoulos, one of the originators of the New America Cinema movement in the 1960s.

Grush then taught at The School of the Art Institute of Chicago, creating a course in film animation in the mid-seventies. He later became an Associate Professor at the College of Art at Northern Illinois University in Dekalb, Illinois, where he taught in the Electronic Media area. He is the author of a book on hand-drawn animation techniques entitled *The Shoestring Animator*. Becoming interested in genealogy, he wrote a trilogy of historical novels based upon what he had learned about his early ancestors.

He and his wife moved to New Mexico in the late 1990s, and opened an art gallery featuring Outsider and Visionary Art in Santa Fe. They returned to the Midwest to retire in the small town of Delavan, Wisconsin, a place that reminds them of their roots. Grush writes, paints and studies Tai Chi.

## Photographs used within the text

The Breakers Hotel. A photochrom postcard published by the Detroit Photographic Company.

William Hale Thompson striking a speaking pose in a room in Chicago, Illinois. Courtesy Chicago Daily News negatives collection, Chicago Historical Society.

Billie Burke in elegant pose in the February 1920 issue of Vanity Fair. Photograph by Baron Adolf De Meyer.

Marjorie Merriweaher Post with her Daughter, 1929. Artist: Giulio de Blaas.

Banyan tree, Palm Beach, Florida, from Robert N. Dennis collection

Mrs. J.J. "Molly" Brown presenting a trophy cup award to Capt. Arthur Henry Rostron, for his service in the rescue of the Titanic. Bain News Service: from the George Grantham Bain collection at the Library of Congress.

Sheriff Robert C. Baker, 1920s.

The Breakers Hotel Fire, March 18, 1925

Howard Philips Lovecraft, around 1915

# Other fiction by Byron Grush

*All The Way By Water*
In which Isaac Grosh brings his wife and eight children to Illinois, traveling by flatboat on the Ohio and Mississippi Rivers.

*Once Upon a Gold Rush*
In which John and James Grosh journey by wagon train to California during the gold rush of '49. Introduces the characters of White Cloud and Little Wind.

*Road of Stars*
In which White Cloud searches for his father (James Grosh) and helps to build the Transcontinental Railroad.

*Dance Beneath A Diamond Sky*
This historical novel of the Sixties follows a group of young people as they search for identity, love, honor and redemption during the decade or so between the assassination of President John F. Kennedy and the resignation of Richard Nixon.

*Romeo's Revenge and Other Wisconsin Stories*
An anthology of twelve short stories about towns and people of Wisconsin.

www.ingramcontent.com/pod-product-compliance
Lightning Source LLC
Chambersburg PA
CBHW060642130626
46555CB00002B/924